Cameron and the Kaiserhof

By the same author

Cameron and the Kaiserhof

Philip McCutchan

St. Martin's Press
New York

Library of Congress Cataloging in Publication Data

McCutchan, Philip, 1920-
  Cameron and the Kaiserhof.

  1. World War, 1939-1945—Fiction.   I. Title.
PR6063.A167C25   1984   823′.914   84-11728
ISBN 0-312-11443-5

First published in Great Britain by Arthur Barker Ltd.

First U.S. Edition

10 9 8 7 6 5 4 3 2 1

1

It had been winter in the South Atlantic, but it was early summer in the UK when Cameron entered Portsmouth, bringing his ship in through the buoyed channel to pass Fort Blockhouse, the submarine base, beneath a clear blue sky with a hint of wind to freshen a warm day. There was no more than a ruffle on the water as the little corvette came through the harbour entrance. England, Cameron thought, looked good. His ship's company thought so too; they were mostly men from the Portsmouth Port Division and there would be wives and girl-friends and mothers not so far away. They wouldn't be waving from the shore as when a ship came home to Pompey after a peacetime commission up the Straits or China-side – in wartime so much secrecy surrounded the movements of HM ships that the families wouldn't even know their menfolk were back; not unless there had been some careless talk in the dockyard . . .

'Berthing signal, sir,' the leading signalman reported as a light began flashing from the signal tower in conveyance of orders from the King's Harbour Master. 'Well, stone me up a gum tree,' the leading signalman said, *sotto voce*. In a louder voice he reported, 'They've bin and gorn and given us the South Railway Jetty, sir!'

Cameron nodded. The flagship berth, reserved in peacetime for the Commander-in-Chief, Home Fleet, flying his flag in the *Nelson* . . . an honour? Hardly. It was just that the big stuff, the battleships and battle-cruisers, had all gone north for the duration to be based in Rosyth and Scapa Flow where they were that much further from the Nazi bombers. So there

1

was plenty of room for a humble corvette commanded by a lieutenant-commander RNVR. Proceeding inwards, coming past HMS *Vernon*, the torpedo school, coming past the Southern Railway's harbour station and the Ryde paddle-steamer waiting to cross Spithead to the Isle of Wight, Cameron took his ship neatly and without fuss alongside the wall. When the lines were ashore and made fast he looked fore and aft along his tiny decks, then nodded at the Officer of the Watch.

'Fall out the hands,' he said.

'Aye, aye, sir.'

'Finished with engines,' Cameron said, passing the order himself down the voice-pipe to the wheelhouse. The cox-swain, who repeated the order to the telegraphsman, had noted a twinge of regret in the Captain's tone. It had been a hard time, down south in the land-locked waters north of Cape Horn, a testing time for any skipper handling his first command, and a strong camaraderie had developed among all hands from bridge to galley, from the Jack Dusty's store to the engine-room, and no one relished the inevitable accompaniment of a return from foreign service – a large number of draft chits. New ships if you got a draft, new faces if you stayed behind. Friendships broken up . . . but never mind, the coxswain said to himself, first things first and he couldn't wait to get leave and be off home to the missus.

A few days later orders came for Cameron while he was on leave with his parents in Aberdeen. He'd intended spending a week at home, then it would be down to London and a girl he'd once known, and a touch of the flesh-pots, or such as a wartime capital could provide in between the many attentions of Goering's *Luftwaffe*. But duty intervened: he was to return to Pompey and hand over his command to an RNR lieutenant and then report soonest possible and in plain clothes to NA2SL – the Naval Assistant to the Second Sea Lord, the fount of all officer appointments, issuing gloom and satisfaction mixed from Queen Anne's Mansions behind Birdcage Walk. And

2

two days later, having said his regretful farewells to the *Briar* and those of her company who had not gone on first leave, he was sitting in Queen Anne's Mansions being briefed by a commander RNVR on NA2SL's staff.

He didn't like what he was hearing. He said, 'I'm no cloak-and-dagger man, sir.'

'It's not exactly cloak-and-dagger.'

'Close enough to it.'

The commander nodded. 'Yes, perhaps. But in the early stages only. The idea's to get to sea as fast as possible. And the matter's urgent.'

Cameron didn't comment; he had not in fact been told very much. His detailed orders, the structure of the work-out, the means of establishing his contacts, would come from a totally unexpected source: Cambridge. He was to report in plain clothes to a don at Emmanuel College. This don was known to Naval Intelligence and to the University as Mr Cambridge; the way in which Cameron was given this information seemed to suggest that the name was cover. This apart, all the commander had revealed was that a German merchant ship was to be cut out from a neutral port and Cameron's job would be to take command of a Naval boarding-party and get the ship away from neutral waters and into the hands of the British Navy. When he enquired as to the urgency, the commander stone-walled, making vague references to operational requirements and the safety of convoys. Cameron's impression was that the commander simply didn't know, and the cloak-and-dagger aspect strengthened in his mind. When the left hand wasn't told what the right hand was doing, the air became thick with intrigue.

He asked one more question. 'Why me, sir? All my experience has been at sea.'

'You've answered your own question, Cameron. We need a good seaman. In some respects you'll be just a passenger until the German's been boarded.' The commander got to his feet and held out his hand. 'Good luck, Cameron. Get up to Cambridge right away. Train from Liverpool Street – leave your gear there. You won't be needing it. Mr Cambridge is

3

expecting you at 1600 hours. Time for tea . . . tea and crumpets in a peaceful Cambridge college, very nice indeed . . . '

And far from the war at sea, Cameron thought. He found a taxi and reached Liverpool Street station just as an air raid was starting. The syrens whined, and people began drifting down into the shelters. No rush; London was used to this. It would be a while yet before the Nazis were overhead if at all – often enough they didn't go where they were expected to. The left luggage office would now be shut; Cameron carried his suitcases down into a shelter and found himself sandwiched between a city man wearing a bowler hat and a cockney woman with five children, three of them snivelling and scared, two of them with a couldn't-care-less aspect. Not all London's children had been evacuated; some mothers just wouldn't part with them, and of those – certainly the vast majority – who had gone in September 1939, a number had come back by this stage of the war, risking the bombs in the interest of getting away from the boredom of the countryside, and the cows, and the mud, back again to the Smoke and mum. One of the two aggressive spirits said in a loud voice, 'Bugger 'Itler.'

The man in the bowler hat winced. 'Language, language,' he reprimanded. 'You should never have heard such a word, boy – '

The mother came to the defence, no delay. 'You shut your bloody trap,' she said shrilly. 'Even 'is late Majesty King George the Fifth said it. Bugger Bognor, 'e said, so I 'eard, *and* in front of Queen Mary, so there!'

The city man flushed and tried to turn his back, but was held fast by a crush of servicemen. London was all uniforms, men on leave, men going on leave or going back to their units, naval drafts on the move through the railway stations, kitbags, hammocks, the soldiers with their rifles and packs, sweating into serge. Soon there was activity: distant crumps and closer explosions and the shelter started to tremble, seemed at one point almost to sway and lift bodily. When the raid was over Cameron emerged to a horrific scene. Steel-

4

helmeted police, ambulances, shattered masonry, fires burning, bodies and a lot of blood. Somewhere people were screaming, and some buildings were still in the process of collapsing. Smoke and dust . . . Cameron put down his suitcases and lent a hand at heavy rescue work until he remembered his orders. There were plenty of willing helpers and Mr Cambridge was waiting. The war had to be fought and that commander had spoken of urgency. In his now torn and scruffy-looking flannel bags and tweed jacket, Cameron carried his suitcases to the left luggage office, now open again for business. The station itself had had little damage and the Cambridge line was open. Cameron caught the first train available in a disorganized time-table. He was going to be late for his tea and crumpets.

Reaching Cambridge station, the longest platform in Britain, Cameron found there were no taxis. He walked down towards St Andrew's Street where he went through an archway into Emmanuel College. Ahead of him was a square of green grass, opposite on the far side of the quadrangle a clock stood above the chapel, surmounted by a weather-vane. The time was 1725. From the porter's lodge on Cameron's right a man emerged, looking him up and down disapprovingly.

'Can I help you, sir?'

'I'm supposed to meet Mr Cambridge – '

'Ah, yes, sir. You'll be – ?'

'The name's Cameron. I know I'm late but I've been in an air raid – '

'Oh, yes, sir, that's why you're a bit messed up.' The porter, who had the air of an ex-RSM, had noted the torn, stained clothing. 'Mr Cambridge has gone out, sir. Said you was to meet him – in a church. Conington, sir. Village about ten miles north-west.'

Cameron stared. 'I'd like to know how I'm to get out there,' he said.

'Car waiting, sir. Mr Cambridge's orders. Out in the street, sir. Local car – Knights Brothers of Fenstanton, what's one-

5

and-a-half miles from Conington. Driver name of Horley. You'll be all right, sir.' The porter went out into St Andrew's Street and lifted an arm. An elderly Morris Cowley came along from near the University Arms Hotel and a tallish man got out when it stopped. He opened the rear door. Cameron got in. Horley got back behind the wheel and drove off towards Petty Cury and Bridge Street, Cameron wondered why a car had been brought so far. It would, he hoped, bring him back to Cambridge again after his meeting in Conington Church, and would then have to drive back on its tracks to its garage in Fenstanton. Talk about waste of precious petrol in wartime, brought across the seas by the tanker crews through trails of death and destruction, braving the U-boats. But his mind was set at some sort of rest when Horley said over his shoulder, 'I understand I'll be taking you on to Huntingdon for the London train, sir.'

Cameron was about to register surprise when he realized that that might not do. The cloak-and-dagger was penetrating already. He said, 'Yes.' He had enough general knowledge of the railway system to know that Huntingdon was on the Kings Cross to Edinburgh line of the London and North Eastern Railway; and knew also that it lay north-west of Cambridge. No waste of petrol after all. But he wished he knew what was going on; he had a suspicion that he wouldn't be taking the train south for London – north for Edinburgh and the Firth of Forth was at least a fifty-fifty chance.

Horley went on, 'I've driven Mr Cambridge all over the place. You'll know, of course, that church monuments are his special interest. Would that be your line too?'

Cameron stifled another wrong response. He said, 'Perhaps it will be when the war's over. I'm certainly interested.'

'There's a lot of history in churches, sir.'

'Yes, that's true.'

Horley was a careful driver. No traffic to speak of, but he didn't exceed thirty miles an hour all the way. At long last the old Morris turned left off the main road and along a narrow country lane with a brook running to the left. At the lane's end they came to an inn called the White Swan and went on through a very small village, a line of cottages on the left and then, past an elm-shaded drive on the right, Cameron saw a stately Georgian building set back in parkland with a yew hedge dividing the gardens from the park.

'The hall,' Horley said. Cameron saw a flag flying from a flagstaff. To his astonishment he recognized it as Polish. He asked what the Poles were doing there.

'The hall was commandeered a year or two ago. I don't know what they get up to there, sir. There's never many troops about. But there's them wireless masts . . .'

Cameron had seen them, poking up from some recently-built Nissen huts. Horley drove on past the hall, took a bend that brought them to the rectory, and then turned up past farm buildings towards the church of St Mary. The car stopped. Horley said he would wait. He got out and opened the door. Cameron walked beneath a lych-gate and along a path to the west door, which stood open. It was a warm evening and the summer scents of the countryside were strong. This was a very remote place . . . Inside a man was standing by the lectern, looking up at one of the many memorials on the walls. Hearing Cameron, he turned. He was a short man in his middle sixties, thickset, and almost entirely bald. To Cameron he hadn't the look of an academic. There was something curiously sinister about him. Perhaps it was the sallow skin and the oddly long neck that seemed to sit uneasily on the short, square body. It was grotesque, almost a deformity, the more so as the head itself was large, giving the neck the appearance of a stalk connecting two boulders.

The man didn't move. Cameron walked up the aisle, feeling a shiver of apprehension run along his spine. 'Mr Cambridge?' he asked.

'That's right.' The voice was a deep rumble, a curious sound to come from so skinny a neck, so meagre an adam's-apple. 'You're Cameron?'

'Yes.'

'Cambridge and Cameron, they go together. Like estate agents, or solicitors, or dentists. Well, well. You're late, damn you, young fellow!'

Cameron explained about the air raid in London. Mr. Cambridge nodded his head, a dangerous-looking manœuvre: the toffee-apple might part from its stick. 'I was going to bring you here in any case. There's someone else you have to meet. He's late too as it happens, but – ' Cambridge broke off. 'You want to know the score, of course. But I'm going to wait till this other man gets here. In the meantime, we'll take a look at the monuments, and you'll appear interested . . . even in these wartime days, the odd tourist drops in, the keen amateur as well as the professional. Not perhaps at this time of day . . . they come on bicycles, you know, and it's mostly this one they want to see.'

Mr Cambridge swept a hand towards a large slab of marble, intricately carved, on the wall to the left of the lectern. 'Grinling Gibbons,' he said.

'Really?'

Cambridge snorted. 'Don't know him from a fried egg, do you? However, he was a master. Carved almost entirely in wood, which is why this marble is of so much interest. And it's signed – d'you see?'

Cameron studied the memorial, which was dedicated to the memory of one Robert Cotton, no more than a youth, who appeared to have been a person of massive attainments, scholarly, kind and humble. A paragon. Cambridge said, 'Look at the others.'

Cameron looked around. Several generations of Philip Thomas Gardners. Other Gardners as well. 'They all seem to be Gardners,' he said. 'Obviously a local family!'

'Yes. Of Conington Hall, as you can see.'

'Squires . . .'

'Yes. It's feudal. Look at the others. Cottons, Askhams, Hattons. All forebears of the Gardners. This whole village is theirs even though they're not in residence any more, victims of the war, of the Polish Army.'

'What are the Poles doing here, sir?'

Slyly Cambridge said, 'Those who don't ask get told no lies, Commander. However, you're going to have to know. The hall's a communications headquarters for the soldiers and naval personnel who got out of Poland, linking all their units presently serving with the British forces.'

'Is that why I'm here?' Cameron asked.

'Not in a direct sense. Still, it's of interest.'

'How indirect, Mr Cambridge?'

Cambridge said, 'We've made an arrangement with the Polish Army. They're going to be our communications link with – what you're going to do. According to the Admiralty, that will help security. Don't ask me how. Admirals are often a curious lot, don't you find? But I suppose there's a certain sense in it, insofar as I'm a frequent and harmless visitor to the village and the church – if you follow what I mean. Also, in the old days before the war, I used to visit the hall. I knew the Gardners, you see. That gave me an accolade . . . the villagers know me and know I'm just a bumbling academic – excellent cover. An old dodderer from Emma.' Mr Cambridge clutched at Cameron's arm. 'I see you're growing more and more curious. You won't have long to wait. I hear someone approaching. There!'

Cambridge was looking towards the door. Cameron turned. A man stood in the porch beneath the belfry. A big man, wearing a badly-fitting sports jacket and light grey trousers with black shoes. On his head was a blue trilby with a wide brim and a feather in the band, the kind of trilby widely advertised before the war as being the Bobby Howes hat. As the man came forward, the hat was removed.

'Mr Cambridge?' the man asked, looking from one to the other.

Cambridge nodded, as dangerously, neck-wise, as before, and turned to Cameron. 'Chief Petty Officer Penrose,' he said. 'Your second-in-command for Operation Highwayman.'

2

Penrose had come by bicycle. He lived in the neighbouring village of Elsworth. He was a Royal Fleet Reservist, having gone out on pension only a year before the start of the war, and he'd joined his brother-in-law in a smallholding. They had marketed pigs in St Ives until the 1939 mobilization of the fleet, when he had been recalled. Currently he was on leave from the Royal Naval Barracks in Devonport; he was a Cornishman, and belonged to the Devonport Port Division. Mr Cambridge told Cameron all this by way of introduction, adding that Penrose was a seaman pure and simple, a salt horse, Chief Bosun's Mate of the battleship *Malaya* before the war. Cameron took to Penrose at first sight: there was a look of solid dependability. An unflappable man with an air of calm authority and confidence.

'And now the details,' Mr Cambridge said, and moved back towards the Grinling Gibbons sculpture. 'First of all, you'll wish to know how I come into this and what my standing is. In point of fact I can't tell you very much about that other than that I come under the Foreign Office umbrella. Because of that, and because of certain contacts through the Special Operations Executive, I have come into possession of certain facts that, surprisingly, were not known – until now – to the Admiralty. Somewhere along the line, and it's a long line, there was . . . shall I say, a break in communications. Someone disappeared. Either killed, or taken into Germany for questioning – most likely the latter.' He paused.

'May we know where from?' Cameron asked.

'Spain. A neutral country very benevolently disposed towards Hitler. Well, we all know that, of course! But the fact is, Spain poses very real problems for the Allies. As a neutral, her neutrality must be respected, even when she is herself in breach of it. You may not agree, Commander. But you'll agree, I think, when I say that Spain must not be brought into the war against us and allowed to provide a direct route to the Straits for Herr Hitler. Gibraltar is of much value, as you know.'

Cameron did. The Gibraltar naval base was vital for the convoy escorts passing through to Malta and Alexandria. Without the Rock's steadfastness the Mediterranean would be wide open to the Nazi U-boat packs, who would join Mussolini's Italian submarine force without hindrance. Mr Cambridge continued. 'Grand Admiral Doenitz is making good use of Spain for Nazi purposes and it is this we have to stop. Spain is riddled with German agents –'

'And with ours, sir?' Penrose asked.

'Not to anything like the same extent, but yes, certainly we have our men *in situ*. The man who disappeared was, of course, one.'

'Yes, sir. Sorry I interrupted, sir.'

'That's all right. You must ask any questions you wish, Penrose – I'm here to answer them. Now, here's the nub of it all. There's a German merchant ship, the former liner *Kaiserhof*, now converted for use as a naval auxiliary, currently in the port of Cadiz on the Atlantic seaboard. More precisely, in the naval dockyard at San Fernando, close to Cadiz. She's being fitted out as a parent ship for midget submarines. Very little is known about these craft except that they each carry a four-man crew – we know nothing about their sea-keeping capabilities, nor their operational range, though we can obviously assume it's enough for their purpose. They pose a very serious threat to the convoys passing through the Straits to and from the Mediterranean and also to those sailing between the UK and Freetown and the Cape. For all we know, their range could conceivably extend to cross the convoy routes well out in the Atlantic.'

11

'Doubtful,' Cameron said.

Cambridge disregarded the comment. He went on, 'We know the Germans are in possession of some very advanced technology and have a lot of special expertise both in men and material – aboard the *Kaiserhof* in San Fernando. We in Britain, as I dare say you know, have made incursions into the midget submarine field, but the Germans are very much more advanced, their craft very much more sophisticated. Our midget submarines are little more than human torpedoes, once-only vehicles for a warhead. The German ones are believed to be capable of more than that. A good deal more.'

Cameron asked, 'Do you know how many they have available?'

'Not precisely, but we believe they have upwards of a hundred, of which around half can be carried at any one time in the *Kaiserhof*'s holds, which have been specially fitted out for the purpose.'

'So they can be launched at sea?'

'Exactly! And the *method* of launch is one of her sophistications. We've not been able to learn all about it, there's a massive degree of secrecy and our one contact actually in the San Fernando dockyard hasn't passed anything through, but it's understood to be a kind of stern launch – rather like the laying of mines, we believe. Anyhow, the ability to launch at sea is a factor that can greatly extend the range, of course. The *Kaiserhof*, you see, isn't comparable with our own submarine depot ships – *Maidstone, Medway, Cyclops* – which remain like mother hens in port awaiting the return of the brood. The *Kaiserhof*,' Mr Cambridge said with the first smile that Cameron had seen on his face, 'is more like a duck. She goes abroad with her lethal ducklings.' The smile faded and he added, 'That is, she will when she's ready.'

'When will that be?'

Cambridge shrugged. 'We don't know. That's one of our difficulties as it happens. I believe you were told at the Admiralty that your job's to cut out the *Kaiserhof* and deliver her to a United Kingdom port?'

'More or less,' Cameron answered. 'It sounds a tall order.

Easier to mount a blockade outside Cadiz – '

'Oh no. Not at all. For one thing: do that, and the *Kaiserhof* wouldn't come out at all. She'd probably send out her midget subs to sink the blockading force, which in any case would be sitting targets for air and surface attack as well –'

Cameron said, 'I know. Only being funny!'

'In any case,' Cambridge went on patiently, 'the whole point really is that special expertise I spoke of, the technology. That's what we want, Cameron. It's your job to get it. You'll not be on your own, naturally. A boarding-party is being sent to Gibraltar independently of you and Penrose . . . and when you bring the *Kaiserhof* out of Cadiz, you'll be met by a cruiser escort from Gibraltar, an escort that will move in at the last moment as advised by yourself on W/T. One of them will put a full steaming-party aboard you for the passage home . . .'

There was a good deal more, mostly about ways and means, the minutiæ of their orders, the establishing of contacts and so on. The cloak-and-dagger atmosphere grew thicker; when they entered Spain from Gibraltar there would be passwords. Mr Cambridge gestured up at the memorial above the lectern. Grinling Gibbons was to be the challenge, Robert Cotton the reply. The first and most vital contact inside Spain would be made with a British agent who would be found playing the piano in a bar in La Linea, the Spanish frontier town and customs post. Mr Cambridge would be manipulating strings from Emmanuel, possibly via Conington Hall's radio network. He refused to be drawn further as to his precise role but Cameron had the idea he was the controller of the Spanish network, the spider that sat in the middle of the web. There was something of the big, square, bloated garden spider in his physique. In the meantime, the immediate orders followed much along the lines that Cameron had foreseen: the route from Huntingdon was north, not south. But not the Firth of Forth. They were to leave the train at York where they would be met by a civilian car and driven to RAF Leeming. They would be flown to Gibraltar kitted out in

13

RAF uniform, a flight lieutenant and a pilot officer. In Gibraltar they would be met by an RAF officer and taken to the officers' mess where more orders would await them.

Walking down the path to the lych-gate, Cameron could scarcely believe what had passed in this small rural village. The soft peace of the summer evening, the song of the birds, the lowing of cattle in the fields, the quiet graves of generations of country people – it was all very far removed from war and the intrigue and danger that inevitably lay ahead. There was a feeling of total unreality. Mr Cambridge, as Cameron and Penrose got into Knights Brothers' car, mounted Penrose's bicycle and pedalled off: he was dining with the rector, who didn't live in Conington's rectory but in that of the twin parish of Fendrayton the other side of the Cambridge road. The bicycle, he said, would be returned to Elsworth next day; and he wished them luck.

In the car they didn't talk much; waiting for the train on Huntingdon platform, they walked up and down together and spoke in low voices. 'What a lark, sir,' Penrose said.

'You'd rather be at sea?'

'Wouldn't you, sir?'

'You can say that again, Chief.' Cameron paused, looking along the railway track that extended dead straight for a long way in both directions. He'd been through this station often enough, going north or south in the Flying Scotsman either as a youth before the war or on leave since: with something of a shock he realized that he'd passed through only the day before, en route from Aberdeen for Portsmouth and the handing over of his sea command. The Navy seemed very far away now. He said, 'Mr Cambridge didn't exactly spell it out, but timing's going to be somewhat vital, Chief. Right?'

Penrose said, 'I reckon I get it, sir. The ship's got to be one hundred per cent ready for sea when we board or else – '

'Or else we'll never get away. And we have to get there before she gets under way on her own account.'

'Tricky, getting it right.'

'And plenty of trickiness in between,' Cameron said. 'For one thing, how do we pass as Spaniards – which it appears is

14

the general idea?'

Penrose grinned and said, 'Just take a good look at me, sir.'

Cameron did so. He said, 'Yes – darkish skin.'

'Cornish, sir. There's still some dark 'uns . . . maybe descendants from Spanish seamen that came to grief on the rocks in years past.'

'Wreckers?'

'Could be, sir. Could be. There was value in the cargoes, and I reckon most Cornishmen have forebears who rigged the false lights to lure the ships on.'

Cameron was looking at him again, eyes narrowed. 'In the right clothes . . .'

'Yes, sir. Dark and swarthy – could pass if we keep our traps shut.'

'We? I doubt if I'd pass for a Spaniard!'

'Spaniards are not *all* darkish, sir. But it's not just the two of us. Look, sir. I was ordered down off leave to be given my orders to rendezvous in that church a couple of miles from home – Elsworth to Conington via Devonport, I ask you – typical of the Andrew, eh? Well, I had a word with the drafting jaunty, he's an old shipmate. Came out in conversation, like, that a lot of Cornish ratings have been mustered the last few days, been formed into a special party to await orders and no more leave given meantime.' Penrose laid a finger against the side of his nose. 'A wink's as good as a nod, they say. And I'm not blind. Or deaf. That's *our* party, getting ready in Devonport. Dark and Cornish! Operation Highwayman . . .'

Cameron said, 'They ought to have called it Operation Wrecker, Chief.'

At RAF Leeming they were provided with their uniforms and issued with basic personal gear – toothbrushes and the like – and with no time lost were embarked aboard a light bomber, a Mosquito, which took off immediately. The dark face of Yorkshire fell away and soon they saw the lighter gleam of the sea far below. They approached Gibraltar at 0800 hours next day, taking a wide sweep to avoid any provocative over-flying

15

of sovereign Spanish territory. Cameron looked down at the massive rock with its big-gun emplacements, its naval dockyard, its military barracks and the clustered white buildings of the town. He looked also at the Spanish mainland beyond the neutral ground and across the great sweep of the bay towards Algeciras, always regarded as swarming with Nazi officers in plain clothes, observing the movements of the British convoys and the disposition of the warships that came and went. There could be no secrecy in or around Gibraltar: everything would be reported back to Berlin where assessments could be made of the numbers of troops on passage and the amount of war supplies being sent through to Malta or further east. North of the bay beyond La Linea rose the great eminence of the Queen of Spain's Chair, a rocky eyrie where Queen Isabella, consort of King Ferdinand, established herself after the capture of Gibraltar by Sir George Rooke in 1704, with the intention of never leaving her seat until the flag of Spain flew once more over the fortress. Chivalrous as ever, the British Governor released her from her vow by obligingly hoisting the Spanish flag until she had climbed down again . . .

'Beer,' Penrose said suddenly.

'Beer?'

'Oceans of it in Waterport Street, sir. Main Street you'll know it as . . . when I first did a commission up the Straits it was called Waterport Street. I could do with a nice pint of Brickwoods.'

'You'll be on plonk before you get a chance to sample the beer, Chief.'

Penrose grimaced. 'Gut rot, is that stuff. Still, it'll have to do, I reckon.'

The airstrip came up below, lethal-looking as the aircraft made its approach. The end of the runway was the Mediterranean: just that. Too much speed and you'd had it. Cameron's heart thumped: he was no air addict. Relief flooded when the Mosquito came to rest. Men came out; there was an RAF officer with a car, obviously on the lookout for Cameron and Penrose. They identified themselves and the RAF officer, a moustachioed flight lieutenant, said it was a good show, and went on to comment that they half expected a prang at each landing. They were taken to the RAF mess where they were given washing facilities and breakfast. After breakfast they were ushered into an office with hard chairs on which they sat in growing impatience for half an hour before someone came in, a man dressed in a well-starched white sharkskin suit and wearing an Old Etonian tie, a tall man with an army look about him.

'Lieutenant-Commander Cameron and Chief Petty Officer Penrose?'

'Yes.' Cameron and Penrose got to their feet but were told to sit again. They did so.

The Old Etonian said, 'I hope you don't mind, but my name doesn't matter. You'll have to take me on trust. Oh – Grinling Gibbons. Right?'

Cameron caught Penrose's eye. There was a snort from the Chief Bosun's Mate, a barely concealed laugh. Cameron, keeping his own face straight with difficulty, said, 'Robert Cotton to you.'

'Good show.' RAF language was catching. 'Now – you know the background so we needn't go into that.' The man sat himself behind the desk that completed the room's meagre furnishings. 'You'll be off into Spain this evening when the dockyard empties. All the Spanish workmen, don't you know. They come and go, morning and evening . . . bloody awful for security but there we are, we couldn't keep the fleet in being without them. Spanish neutrality's a flimsy thing that works both ways at once. Don't interrupt me, please,' he said as Cameron's mouth opened. 'You may ask questions later. The workmen. Damn useful at times like this, don't you know – we can infiltrate whoever we want and believe me, we do. They know it, of course. Not individuals, I don't mean that, you'll be perfectly all right, but the *fact* that we do is well known – obviously. They do it the other way round, the difference being that mostly we know *who* they've sent in and we react accordingly – false leads, you know the sort of thing. Bum information. The whole situation's a joke really. Not so far as you're concerned I need hardly say. Now – when you're

17

across the frontier, dressed as Spanish workmen, you contact a man called Pedro Gomez, I say again Pedro Gomez, not hard to remember – I won't tell you his real name, but he's as English as I am – in the Granada Bar not far from the *aduana*, customs post that is. Turn right into a cobbled square. Questions?'

'Will he,' Cameron asked solemnly, 'be playing a piano?'

'Yes, as a matter of fact he will.' Light blue eyes opened in a wide stare and the head was held back. 'May I ask how you knew that, Cameron?'

'I was told.'

'In London?'

'No, in –'

'Don't mention that. Not even in this room. We're *never* precise. All right, so you know. Well now. You may wonder how you're going to cope with the local dialect, the Andalusian. It's very different from Castillian. You speak Castillian?'

'No,' Cameron said, 'no Spanish at all. Didn't they tell you?'

'They didn't, but it's not important. We knew all along it wouldn't be possible to find enough naval personnel who could speak Spanish *and* take a ship out. That's been coped with. In the first instance it'll be coped with by a person, an RNVR lieutenant who *does* speak Andalusian, who'll cross with you, also disguised as a dockyard workman. He's a lieutenant of the Special Branch,' he added. 'Not a seaman. And he knows Pedro Gomez, so you'll have no difficulty there. Further questions?'

'Topography,' Cameron said. 'Routes. A detailed description of Cadiz and its approaches and the San Fernando dockyard. Weapons and –'

'Yes, yes. Quite. Gomez will provide all necessary detail. He's also providing all you'll need in the way of weaponry. First get to Gomez. Take it a step at a time, that's my advice, it's the only way. I gather neither of you has done this sort of thing before?'

'That's right, we –'

'Very good experience. You'll learn a lot. Now, once

you've boarded the *Kaiserhof* and secured control – '

'Just one moment,' Cameron interrupted. 'How large is my boarding-party to be?'

'I haven't the details of that,' was the somewhat huffy answer. 'That's a Naval matter, but I'm certain you'll have enough men for the purpose – '

'And the *Kaiserhof*'s complement?'

That, it appeared, was known. 'Three hundred in the ship's company, plus the midget submarine crews. Say another two hundred. It may sound heavy odds against your likely number, but you should have the advantage of surprise and you'll be well armed – and I know from experience what a handful of men with automatic weapons can achieve when they have the element of surprise in their favour. And of course your steaming-party will be put aboard you from the cruisers once you're out past Cadiz. Now, what was I saying?' He seemed put out.

Cameron said. 'Once I've secured control.'

'Oh yes. Well, once you've done that and are ready for sea, you're to use the ship's wireless transmitter to call Flag Officer Gibraltar. You make the two words Grinling Gibbons in plain language – that's all. That's the signal you're about to move out from San Fernando, which is the naval dockyard for Cadiz, as I dare say you know. You'll get no acknowledgement, but you can rely upon it, a cruiser squadron will meet you just outside Spanish waters. From then on you'll come under the orders of the Rear-Admiral commanding the cruisers. I think that's all.'

Glancing at his wrist-watch, the military-looking man got to his feet. He said, 'Wait here,' and left the room, briskly, seeming almost to march himself out. Chief Petty Officer Penrose was looking more and more uneasy, more and more displeased with an unwelcome draft. Cameron felt much the same and understood only too well. For part of the flight from RAF Leeming, until sleep had overtaken them, he had talked to Penrose. Penrose was a man who loved the sea and had been glad enough to get back to the service when his recall had come. Elsworth, the smallholding and St Ives market

19

were all very well and he knew he'd been lucky to drop into an open-air life, but the sea was in his blood. His father and both grandfathers had been fishermen, working out of Penzance. He himself had joined the Navy as a seaman boy just before the 1914–18 war, when Edward VII had been not long dead. He had memories of Lord Fisher and the Dreadnoughts, and had served throughout the Great War in the ships of the Grand Fleet under both Jellicoe and Beatty. As a young able seaman he had been at the Dogger Bank and Jutland, on the latter occasion aboard the fleet flagship *Iron Duke*. In all his service career he had done little time in barracks or other shore establishments. He had taken no specialist courses: his non-substantive rating was that of seaman gunner, the most basic of all. His skills lay in seamanship pure and simple, a commander's right-hand man when it came to upper-deck work, boats, rigging, anchors and cables and the making of other men into seamen by example and leadership. He wasn't going to like threading his way through Spain keeping, as he had said already, a shut trap. No more was Cameron.

They were not kept waiting long. Another civilian came into the room and took them out to a waiting car that drove them past the Land Port and along Main Street to enter the dockyard by the Ragged Staff gate.

That evening, for some while before the hooter went to signal the end of the day's work in the dockyard, the Spanish workmen had been queuing up in a long, shuffling line. Cameron and Penrose were among them, indistinguishable from the rest even down to a couple of bags of sugar and coffee concealed in their denim trousers; the Spanish officials at the *aduana* turned blind eyes to a little smuggling and were not averse to a handout themselves, such was the shortage of certain commodities in Spain. Not to smuggle might attract attention; and Lieutenant Hanbury of the RNVR's Special Branch, the officers who wore a green stripe between the gold on their sleeves and whose designation covered a whole miscellany of duties ranging from meteorology to mine countermeasures and occasionally intelligence work, was similarly equipped. Hanbury was a morose individual with a long, dark face, tallish and as thin as a skeleton. He was some years older than Cameron. He spoke the Andalusian dialect like a native, having spent a couple of pre-war years in Granada and Malaga researching into gypsies and flamenco dancing. He was a writer on these subjects; and there was nothing of the Navy about him. Now he was being a shepherd, shuffling along in the apparently endless queue of Spaniards behind Cameron and Penrose, all ready to speak on their behalf if any questions should be asked.

'Not that there'll be any,' he'd said earlier while their disguise was being assumed. 'The blokes at the *aduana* aren't all that hot. Nor all that interested. All you do is sort of flip your card at them – they don't even bother to look. It's just their daily chore and the sooner it's over the sooner they can slack right off again. Spain's like that.'

'I hope it's like it all the way to Cadiz,' Cameron said.

Hanbury laughed. 'It will be, don't worry. That is, unless we come up against any Nazis. That'll be different.'

Cameron had asked about the rest of the party, having in mind what Penrose had said in regard to Party Highwayman being mustered in Devonport barracks. Hanbury told him they were being flown out and would filter across the frontier during the next two days. He understood that twenty-five men had been detailed, mostly seamen, though there would be a leading telegraphist and a Chief Engine-Room Artificer to take charge below with the assistance of an ERA, a Stoker Petty Officer, two leading stokers and an electrical artificer. 'Carefully chosen,' he said. 'Dyed-in-the-wool Cornishmen.' His face lit in a brief smile. 'Pirates,' he said. He added that the steaming-party that would be put aboard outside Cadiz would be fully adequate to take the *Kaiserhof*, under Cameron's command, to her UK destination, probably the Clyde. This steaming-party would consist of four executive officers, three engineer officers and forty-eight ratings of the seaman and engine-room branches plus a couple of stewards and three cooks. Also three signalmen.

It had been shortly after this conversation that they had

21

joined the queue. It was a hot evening, stifling, with no wind to move the air. There was a strong smell of garlic and sweat that was not wholly overlaid by the usual dockyard aromas of oil fuel and tar. Dust was everywhere. From the military barracks around the Rock bugles blew. Gibraltar Bay was a shimmer of purple, stretching across to the Spanish shore. The destroyers forming the Force H escort lay at the pens, getting steam up for sea. Departure imminent . . . There was a Colony class cruiser in the graving-dock, two other cruisers and an aircraft carrier at the moles. As the queue moved on, coming out of the dockyard gate, faster now that the hooter had sounded, Cameron looked back. Gibraltar, though the army and the RAF might not agree, was all Navy, the Rock itself eloquent of Britain's sea power, of the command of the sea exercised for so many years past. In Spain they would at least be doing something to help in keeping it intact.

3

They passed across the airstrip and through the British frontier control into the neutral zone, the no man's land that lay between the Rock and Spain; and thence through the gates where the *aduana* was situated. Civil Guards lounged, carrying rifles and wearing the traditional shiny, flat-backed caps above the light greenish-blue uniforms, largely dirty. One or two smoked cigarettes; there was some badinage with the workmen. None of the British party was spoken to. The whole thing was dead easy.

They moved to the right away from the customs post, entering the cobbled square that the military-looking man had mentioned. The Granada Bar was at the far end of the square, a biggish place compared with the other bars. Tables were set outside and the sound of music came from within, guitars and a piano. The place was crowded; Penrose and Cameron sat at one of the two unoccupied tables outside; from a waiter Hanbury ordered glasses of Fundador, the brandy of Spain, before going into the bar. He was gone for only a short while; the piano continued while he was absent. When he returned he said nothing of any consequence but chatted of this and that in his fluent Andalusian, his expression giving the others the cue when to nod, or laugh, or shake their heads. The drinks finished, he got to his feet. Cameron and Penrose followed suit. Under Hanbury's guidance they left the square and entered a narrow alley running between close-set, crumbling dwellings. Cameron asked no questions; he felt utterly out of his element. The idea as he understood it had been to meet Pedro Gomez in the Granada Bar. But no

23

doubt Hanbury knew what he was doing.

He did. As they came out of the square he murmured, 'Too chancy. There was a German in there.'

'You didn't contact Gomez?'

'Yes, I did. Just a word and a slap on the back, you know the sort of thing. Old mates. He'll be along within a couple of hours.'

'Where?'

'Where he lives. It won't be up to much, but it's home to Gomez. Just while he's in Spain.'

'What about the German?' Cameron asked.

'What about him?'

'Does it mean trouble?'

'I doubt it. It just wasn't the moment to talk, that's all. The sods are everywhere, no reason why one shouldn't be in the Granada. They're having a lovely soft war one way and another.'

'They'll be having the *Kai* – '

'All right, hold it. There are some things we don't mention, just in case. That's one.'

So would be Conington Hall and the Polish radio link, so would be Mr Cambridge. Cameron took what amounted to a rebuke from a subordinate in silence; he had much yet to learn and this wasn't the time to labour rank. The place where Gomez lived was some distance from the bar and Cameron was soon lost geographically in a maze of criss-cross streets and alleys. When they reached Gomez' abode it was no more than a room in what appeared to be a brothel. Men were coming and going, there was a smell of cheap scent and from a balcony above a female gestured down into the alley. Hanbury returned the gesture together with some Spanish and the woman scowled briefly and disappeared. The three of them went through a doorway into a narrow, smelly hall with stairs rising steeply at the end. The room occupied by Pedro Gomez was on the left of the entry, and Hanbury pushed open the door and went in followed by the others.

They had a longish wait for Gomez to turn up.

When he came he was a short, swarthy man with black hair

24

and a limp. Cameron would have taken him for a genuine Spaniard anywhere, let alone here in the frontier town. Gomez insisted on the passwords, which were exchanged. When he spoke his English was heavily accented. He had, he said, lived for many years in Spain, for longer in fact than he had lived in England, and Spanish was by now his normal tongue. He was basically a journalist; but currently, as cover for his activities for the Foreign Office, he worked by day in the cork woods between La Linea and Algeciras and by night as the pianist in the Granada Bar.

'I commute by bicycle,' he said. 'The exercise is good. Now. You will wish for the details, Commander.' Cameron was having difficulty in hearing him: before he had opened his mouth, Gomez had switched on a portable, battery-fed radio and music was blaring out to cover his words. 'You will need to be patient in the first instance. You will move from here soon after midnight, but then there will be a delay that can't be helped. More men will be joining –'

'Yes. Hanbury told me that. Will they come here?'

Gomez nodded. 'They will, but not all at once. There might be suspicions. They will come in small groups, and they will be forwarded to the place you yourself are going to. When they have all reported, then you will move on. I shall come myself to tell you the next step when all are present. For now, I shall go into the overall workout only. You know, of course, what it is you have to do. I have to tell you that time may be short and once all the boarding-party are with you, you'll have to move fast.' He paused. 'I've had fresh intelligence from Cadiz. And at the same time, news from – elsewhere. Taken together, it's not too reassuring. Do you know anything of forthcoming fleet movements, Commander?'

Cameron shook his head. 'No, I don't.'

'Then you won't know that a United States Task Force is due to pass through the Straits shortly?'

'No. When?'

'On the twenty-third, which is just six days from now. They're going through to the Middle East – joining up with our Eastern Mediterranean Fleet ready to back up a maritime operation in the Piræus.' Gomez gave Cameron a quizzical look. 'I don't suppose you knew *that* was on, either. I need hardly add, the information's top secret as the Americans say. But no doubt you can estimate how vital it is our friends in Cadiz don't get away to sea. We believe they're well aware of the movements of the Task Force . . . and my new information from certain persons in Cadiz is that they'll be all ready to go in good time to have the ducklings in position to attack the American ships. The Task Force consists of the battleships *North Dakota, South Carolina, Nevada* and *Wyoming*, with an aircraft carrier and a destroyer escort – '

'I imagine they've been warned?'

Gomez said, 'As a matter of fact, they haven't. You know as well as I do, the security of our codes and cyphers is not to be relied on one hundred per cent. If they're cracked, then the Nazis will know that information about Cadiz has leaked to us. We don't want that – they have to be lulled for as long as possible, right to the end in fact, or we won't have a hope.'

'But look here – '

Gomez interrupted flatly. 'You heard. The orders come from on high. In any case, the Americans have an anti-submarine screen and can be relied on to make good use of it. If they don't, well, then, it's their lookout.' He paused. 'That sounds harsh. So is war. And I have to admit that if these midget subs attack in strength, no destroyer screen's going to keep them all out. Hitler doesn't mind losing half, just so long as the other half gets through. It's up to you to see none of them leaves Cadiz – that's all!'

Cameron caught his CPO's eye: Penrose was looking grim. It was a tall order. Gomez went into the details of the operation while he prepared supper on a filthy oil stove in one corner of his room. Supper consisted of some sort of soup, lentil Cameron believed, with stale bread and a little rindy cheese, all washed down with a bottle of the local vino. Gomez, as he doled out the soup, said that when they reached their next stopover they would find revolvers, hand grenades and sub-machine guns, enough for the whole party. There would be sufficient ammunition for the assault on the

26

Kaiserhof and to hold the German crew prisoner thereafter. He anticipated no difficulty in getting the party to the Cadiz area. Entering the San Fernando dockyard would be more difficult. Being a naval yard it was well guarded, and there would be plenty of Germans in the vicinity of the *Kaiserhof*. Boldness or subterfuge – Cameron would have to make his choice when he had assessed the situation. The run through from the port past Cadiz itself to the open sea would be hazardous, but there was a fair chance that if Cameron could keep a degree of silence aboard after his apparently Spanish party had climbed the gangways, the shoreside Nazis might not realize that their pride and joy was in enemy hands. And even if they ticked over as a result of any necessary shooting aboard, then they might not take too kindly to the idea of the Spanish guns pumping away into the *Kaiserhof*, by that time loaded with her complement of midget submarines and their crews. In any event a certain amount of confusion ashore could be relied upon.

'Nelson,' Gomez remarked, 'would have relished it.'

Soon after midnight transport arrived in the alley: three donkeys – four if that belonging to the man who was to guide the party was counted. The guide was one of the Allied network – a Frenchman from the Pyrenees, a Gaullist with perfect Spanish and an undying hatred for the Nazis, who had shot up his family in their home in a village in the foothills. His cover name was Juan Espeso, a man who made his living by cultivating and selling almonds. The donkeys carried panniers lately filled with his produce, now emptied after a good day's trade in La Linea.

Saying goodbye to Pedro Gomez, they trundled off along the alley, making for the high road running down to Algeciras by way of San Roque. There was a high moon; Gibraltar stood out clearly with its many lights climbing the sides of the Rock. There was no wartime blackout for the Rock, which couldn't be hidden in any case, with the moon silvering the sea all round and the lights of La Linea pointing it up. And in fact there had been only one air raid since the start of the war, and that had been in daylight – it had come not from the Germans or Italians but from French aircraft after the British attack on the *Richelieu* at Dakar. The waters of the bay lay placid and shining beneath the moon. Everything was peace except for the busy movement of the Navy's patrol boats guarding the harbour and its approaches.

Once again Cameron had time on his mind. If the US Task Force was expected to pass through the Straits in six days from now, then the *Kaiserhof* could equally be expected to clear away to sea possibly two days before that so as to have her midget submarines on station well outside the narrows.

Four days. Two, from the time the party was complete and they left the first stopover.

Well, that should be more than enough to reach the vicinity of Cadiz, of course. The distance was only around ninety miles. On the other hand the roads would be poor and there might be Spanish military or naval traffic on them – Gomez had said as much. Progress could be slow if they had to take to the country to avoid trouble, but Cameron hoped to reach his destination with plenty of time in hand. There would be transport laid on, motorized transport. Gomez had been no more precise than that. Cameron could only hope it would take them all the way. If there were road blocks they might have to abandon the transport and leg it. Also, Spanish transport other than the ubiquitous donkey tended to be unreliable according to Gomez, and Hanbury too. Breakdowns were frequent and garages few, though the Spanish lorry drivers could always be relied upon to render roadside assistance and possibly to give a tow . . .

They reached San Roque, a town set upon a hill. Few lights: the people were mostly in bed, peacefully sleeping. The moon silvered the road as it had the sea. From San Roque the road ran south to Algeciras and thence Cadiz, the only road from La Linea to the naval base. After San Roque they entered a tiny village, a scatter of dwellings – Guadacorte, on First River. To the left of the road, their guide said, was a farm. This was part of a large estate in British ownership, the property of the Marquess of Bute. The workers on the estate were very pro-British and there was a safe refuge for their purposes. The Frenchman led the party off the main road and along a narrow track running in a twist between eucalyptus and olive trees and a number of cork oaks. Here the moon was partially obscured but although the way was dark the donkeys kept as if by instinct to the track, never once stumbling against the close trees.

At the track's end a building loomed through the darkness. At first Cameron fancied it was a house; but as they came close he saw that it was a shed built of wood, with a wooden slatted roof.

The guide halted and slid from his donkey. '*Voilà*,' he said, pointing to the shed. Hanbury had words with him, then gave Cameron the gist. 'He says no one comes here and we'll be totally secure. But no chances even so. He and I will work in two watches, keeping handy just in case someone happens along. If they do, we'll deal with them.'

'How?'

Hanbury shrugged. 'Soft words of peace and goodwill – and a convincing explanation. If it fails to convince . . . well, then there's this.'

He brought a long thin knife from the band of his trousers. Cameron, in a shaft of moonlight filtering through the cork oaks, saw the gleam. The knife looked deadly, would penetrate fast and with ease. He hoped it wouldn't have to be used on a Spaniard. To be clandestinely in a neutral country was bad enough; to kill one of its citizens could precipitate almost anything. It was in fact one of the things he had put to Mr Cambridge in the church at Conington. Cambridge had said he was to keep his eyes on the main target: the *Kaiserhof*. He had been no more precise than that. The Foreign Office had never been keen to commit itself if it was possible to avoid it. Nevertheless the sentiment was clear enough. So was its corollary: if Cameron failed and was taken, he and Party Highwayman would be out on a limb of their own.

He asked about the guns and ammunition referred to by Gomez. The Frenchman understood his question, put in English to Hanbury for interpretation. Using English himself, the guide said, 'In the shed – you will see. Come, follow, please.'

They did. They went into the shed, which smelled of cut wood and the bark of the oaks that made the cork. The Frenchman, bringing a small torch from a pocket, went over to a pile of planks and other timber. He shifted some of it, assisted by the three British. As the pile was cleared, a trapdoor was revealed. This trapdoor was set right into the earth. The Frenchman lifted it with some difficulty and shone the torch down. Cameron and the others saw a hole some three feet deep, lined with planking and excavated out sideways at the bottom. Craning his neck Cameron saw the dull gleam of gunmetal in the light from the torch.

'You are satisfied?'

'Short of bringing them all up and examining them – yes.'

'For now, they are better where they are, m'sieur. When we move again, then will be the time. Until then we cover them again.'

They did so, more lightly than before. A need for them could come before they moved on. The Frenchman shifted the beam of his torch on to a corner of the shed. Cameron saw a sizeable tank, square and made of what he believed to be galvanized iron. It had a lid with a hasp and padlock. The Frenchman said, 'In there is food and containers of water. It must be rationed. I shall ration it. I have the key. There are also Spanish cigarettes.' Gomez had already said no English cigarettes were to be smoked, no contact with Gibraltar or its dockyard indicated in the future. 'Now you shall sleep while I keep watch.'

He extinguished the torch and went outside.

Cameron had been asleep for little more than a matter of minutes when he came suddenly awake. There had been a sound, something outside. Penrose had also woken.

'What was that, sir?'

'I don't know. I thought I heard someone cry out.'

Followed by Penrose, he padded softly to the door.

4

Outside there was silence. The moon gave patchy light, not very much. Nothing stirred as Cameron edged the door open, quietly and cautiously. He was aware of Hanbury waking and coming up behind him and peering out over his shoulder as he opened the door wider. Then he saw something move, something indistinct in a patch of moonlight, down along the track from the main road.

He came out from the shed. Hanbury pushed past him unceremoniously and he caught the gleam of steel, the knife held by the Special Branch lieutenant. Cameron's first instinct was to stop any killing. But Hanbury knew this sort of work better than he did. He could probably be relied on not to kill unless it was vital – and in any case he had gone forward like a cat, making no sound and keeping hidden in the shadows and the trees.

'Follow on, sir?' Penrose said in a hoarse whisper.

Cameron nodded. They moved away from the hut, keeping for the time being to the track. Cameron felt the thud of his heart: to strike trouble at this stage, perhaps to run into Germans or be arrested by the Spanish military or police . . . that didn't bear thinking about. Feeling that the whole operation could now be in jeopardy, he moved ahead. He had gone around twenty yards from the shed when he saw something just off the track, in amongst the trees, visible in a sliver of moonlight.

A man's feet, motionless and lying oddly.

He stopped. With Penrose he moved off right. He bent down by the feet. The moon flickered through the trees. He recognized the French guide. Penrose knelt and ran his hands over the man. Then he said, 'Dead, I reckon. No heartbeat.'

Cameron moved forward. Laying a hand in the vicinity of the heart, he could only confirm what Penrose had said. As his hands touched the face, he found the flesh bloated and somehow with a soggy feel. When he felt around the neck he found thin wire, very tightly drawn.

He stood up. 'Strangled,' he said in a hard voice. 'Snared. Like a rabbit. Just like a rabbit caught by a poacher.'

Penrose said, 'Bloody Nazis.'

'We don't know that, Chief.'

'No, sir, we don't know. All the same . . . where's Mr Hanbury got to, eh?'

'Don't ask me!'

'Let's hope he gets the bugger that did this lot,' Penrose said, sounding savage. 'Do we leave the Frenchie where he is, sir, or what?'

'Leave him for the time being. He'll have to be hidden soon.' He stiffened. 'D'you hear anything, Chief?'

'Not a thing, sir . . . wait a minute, though. I reckon – '

'Someone coming,' Cameron whispered. 'Keep dead still, Chief.' No weapons: just their fists. He was aware of Chief Petty Officer Penrose flexing his muscles. He was a big man and hadn't gone to fat. He'd told Cameron he'd once been heavyweight champion of the Navy, possibly too many years ago now, when he'd been a PO, captain of the foretop in the old battleship *Resolution*. But he could still fight with the best, or so he reckoned. Any moment now, he might be able to prove it. But the slight sound was Lieutenant Hanbury coming back. Cameron and Penrose relaxed as the lieutenant came into the moonlight.

Cameron said, 'Someone got the Frenchman.'

'I know. And I got the someone.' There was satisfaction in Hanbury's voice. He jerked a hand over his shoulder. 'He's back there. I'll need a hand to bring him in. 'All right?'

Cameron nodded. 'What is he? Spanish?'

'I don't think so,' Hanbury said. 'He doesn't smell like a Spaniard. He smells like a German. You know what I mean –

32

sauerkraut, apfelstrudel, sausage and beer. If I was to add the smell of concentration camps . . . well, I'd be using my imagination. But somehow the aura's there. Let's get busy.'

Hanbury turned away. Cameron felt slight irritation at the way Hanbury seemed to be taking charge, never making even a pretence of deferring to someone who was in fact his senior officer. But the irritation didn't last. Hanbury was older and this was, after all, a special operation in which he, Cameron, was totally inexperienced. He recalled, as he followed close behind Hanbury and moved as silently as possible through the trees, that the Old Etonian in Gibraltar – or had it been Mr Cambridge? – had said that he would be little more than a passenger until the boarding-party had taken over the *Kaiserhof*. That would be when his time would come.

Ahead of him, Hanbury slowed to a stop. His track back to the dead man had been unerring. With Penrose he bent down. They lifted the body and retraced their steps. They stopped briefly by the body of the Frenchman and Hanbury felt in the pockets for the man's torch, which he removed. Then they took up the burden again. When the body was in the shed, Cameron went back with Penrose for the Frenchman and carried him inside.

They found Hanbury examining the other body in the light of the torch.

'Well?' Cameron asked.

Hanbury was frowning. He didn't answer right away, but went on staring down at the body. It was short, thickset, with broad shoulders and something of a stomach. A beer gut, as Penrose remarked.

'Yes,' Hanbury said. 'You're right. Got in a Berlin beer hall, I shouldn't wonder. A pound to a penny he's a Hun.' He looked up at Cameron. 'I've checked right through. No documentation, nothing personal even – just nothing at all. Travelled light, it seems. Except for this.'

He held up a small automatic pistol. '6.35mm. Handbag stuff, but often quite useful.'

'German?'

'No, it's an Italian job. That doesn't have to mean anything at all, of course. Anyway, it's his total luggage – except for that revolting snare. Now we'd better shove 'em both down the ammunition hole.'

'And seal in the guns?'

'Can you suggest anywhere better?'

Cameron shrugged. 'No, I can't. All right, then, let's get it over.'

'I hope we're not here too long,' Hanbury said with a grimace. 'Hot countries . . . they don't suit the dead.'

Later they discussed the implications. Cameron was worried that the facts of Operation Highwayman might have blown. Hanbury didn't think so. 'Not necessarily,' he said. 'I admit there's a risk, of course. But something tells me this could have been a personal thing.'

'Just a feud?'

'Well, in the broad sense, yes. But I don't mean they'd fallen out over a señorita, that sort of thing. I mean the Hun could have got to know our Frenchman wasn't what he made himself out to be – a simple Spanish *hombre* engaged in cultivating almonds. No – a Gaullist agent was being despatched – by order of the Führer, ultimately. Anyway, that's what I think.'

'Any special reason?'

Hanbury put a finger against the side of his nose and said solemnly, 'Just a kind of instinct. I have a nose for these things – we all cultivate it eventually. You *have* to. If you don't, you don't survive. You haven't got it yet.'

'Thanks,' Cameron said drily.

'I don't mean to be depressing. If I have been, I apologize. And if you want hard reasons, I can offer only this: if the Nazi agents here in Andalusia had wind of Highwayman, they wouldn't have sent a lone bod in at this stage. They would have waited to nab the lot, probably in Cadiz. Catch us all *in flagrante delicto*. Nice propaganda point for use with the neutrals, or such as there are in this bloody war.'

'Which they may yet do.'

'Yes, indeed, which they may yet do. But not this time. Now I think we all need some sleep.'

Hanbury rolled over on the earth floor and was soon asleep. He seemed unconcerned about maintaining the watch outside, possibly feeling that an attempt having been made – and made successfully up to the point of the attacker's own death – no one else would be bothering them in the very few hours now left until the dawn.

Hanbury seemed to have nerves of steel. But Cameron decided to maintain a lookout on his own. Penrose wanted to take his turn and had to be ordered to catch up on his sleep. Cameron went outside and kept watch on the track and the nearer trees. Already the darkness was tending to lift, to be less thick and black; and soon dawn came, peacefully, with delicate colours to fill the sky with green and mauve and blue to herald another day of southern Spain's blistering summer heat.

The following night the next instalment of Party Highwayman in Gibraltar was sent through by Gomez. Stoker Petty Officer Tremain, only recently of RNB Devonport and basically from the Cornish fishing village of Polruan, said, 'Jeepers creepers, what a pong.' He came further into the shed, holding his nose. He was confronted by Cameron, Hanbury and Penrose. 'What's all this?' he asked briskly, then coughed. 'Sorry. One of you's Lootenant-Commander Cameron I don't doubt?'

'Yes,' Cameron said. 'And you?'

'Stoker PO Tremain, sir – '

'Glad to have you with us, PO.'

'Glad to join – I s'pose, sir.' Tremain gave an ostentatious sniff. 'Done any killing recently, sir?'

It was Hanbury who answered, in a tone that didn't invite further questions. 'Yes.'

The Stoker PO looked startled. He called the roll of his companions. 'Leading Telegraphist Bolus, sir. Leading Stokers Treffry and Poldean.' He went through the list: the rest of the newly-joined detachment included six seaman ratings, one of them a leading seaman named Warlock, an RFR man whom Chief Petty Officer Penrose greeted as an old shipmate; they'd done a commission together China-side years before in the cruiser *Hawkins*. All told the party consisted of eleven men, the last being an electrical artificer, the only non-Cornish rating, EA Lampton. They were accompanied by another guide, a British agent who told Cameron that the remainder would join the next night and would be brought by Pedro Gomez himself, after which the whole party would move out for San Fernando. Cameron reported the facts of the previous night and asked what was to be done about the bodies.

'You'll have to bury them,' the agent said.

'We might be heard.'

'You've just got not to be, that's all! Use some of the timber here to dig with – the planks – that shouldn't make too much noise. Shallow graves . . . but well covered up afterwards. This place might be checked over for all we know – we can't take the risk. But first I'll take a look at your suspected Jerry.'

Penrose detailed two of the seamen to clear away the clutter from above the trapdoor. The lid was lifted; the stench came up more strongly, almost overpoweringly. With a handkerchief clamped over his nostrils, the man from La Linea peered down, using a torch. He was unable to see the German properly; the Frenchman's body was on top of it. He lowered himself down, shifted the bodies a little, gave an exclamation and heaved himself back to the lip of the pit, looking sick. As he stood up he said, 'He's a Nazi all right. I recognized him. Gestapo, from Algeciras. A nasty bugger, name of Sturmer.'

'Any connexion with Cadiz?' Cameron asked.

The agent shook his head. 'Not so far as I know, but it's not to be banked on. We're pretty confident nothing's leaked about the cutting-out operation, but this could cause trouble.'

'You mean he'll be looked for,' Hanbury said. 'We realized that, of course, assuming he was a Nazi. But I imagine there's no reason for them to come looking around here?'

'Not unless he told someone what he was doing last night. Knowing Sturmer, he probably didn't. He was always up to something on his own.'

36

'Something his bosses didn't know about?'

There was a shrug from the agent. 'Could be, on occasions.' Hanbury glanced at Cameron: his own earlier theory about a private war against the Gaullist could have been correct. 'Mostly his idea was to bring something off on his own. Steal a march, get noticed by Himmler. He felt he was a little out of the main stream of promotion, I fancy.'

'So if that's right,' Hanbury said, 'it looks as though we're safe. Or as safe as we're going to be.'

'That's right,' the agent answered, and turned to Cameron. 'You'd better get busy on burial parties, old man. And sooner you than me!'

Cameron grimaced. 'Are you going back to La Linea?' he asked.

'Yes. I shall be reporting to Gomez, of course. If there's any change in the plans as a result of last night – which I doubt – I'll let you know. In the meantime, stay put. But keep a careful lookout right the way through.'

As the British agent left for La Linea Leading Seaman Warlock took charge of the grave-digging party, which besides himself consisted of all five seaman ratings plus one of the leading stokers, Treffry. Treffry came from Bodmin. A short, wiry man, he had been in the army pre-war – the Duke of Cornwall's Light Infantry, whose short, fast marching step suited short men. It made tall men look ridiculous and was highly uncomfortable. Treffry had served on the North-West Frontier of India with the DCLI and hadn't liked it, which was why he'd left as soon as his short-service engagement with the Colours had expired, after which he'd joined the Andrew, just before the war. One reason he hadn't liked the army was that men died from time to time when out on patrol, either from the *jezails* of the local Pathan banditry or from disease, always rife in India, and they had had to be buried. . .

Private Treffry as he then was had on two occasions taken part in digging shallow graves to be surmounted with small cairns of stones. He hadn't liked it; it was hard work to start with, but more importantly it brought cruelly home the simple fact of man's mortality, that he might be the next one to go and that he would be left there beneath the fierce Indian sun, in a rugged and hostile land where the vultures hovered and uttered their harsh, hungry cries. He found it all very depressing.

He hadn't expected to have to dig graves in the Andrew. In the Andrew, the sea was the natural resting-place for the dead. He uttered sour comments as he dug a piece of timber into the hard ground. He made them until he was told *sotto voce* by the Stoker PO to bloody shut up. Leading hands shouldn't moan, the Stoker PO said, it wasn't setting a good example.

'It's not a stoker's work, isn't this, PO,' Treffry objected.

'You're not a stoker now, lad, you're part of something different. We all pull together, see.'

'Or bloody dig together, more like.' Viciously in the patchy moonlight that had returned with the night, Leading Stoker Treffry dug again and shifted some more earth. This was going to take till dawn, the more likely so as the officer kept on nattering about keeping it quiet. Roll on my bleeding twelve, Treffry thought, and may the rest of the twelve be served at sea. Preferably based on Guz: Treffry had a girl-friend in Bodmin, not all that far from Devonport by train or bus, who worked in the bar of the Duke of Cornwall public house. On the stout side, she was comfortable and motherly, which Treffry liked, having never known his own mother. He'd been one of the abandoned babies, left on the step of a public house named the Treffry Arms, hence his name. It had been the orphanage authorities that had made him join the perishing army as a boy soldier, and sod them for that. Treffry dug and thrust with his piece of wood. Cameron had chosen sites as free as possible of the trees, but even so the ground seemed to be all roots.

Treffry's next lunge slid off rather more than the root of a tree and this caused him to lose his balance. He fell flat, which was just as well for everyone else, for what his piece of timber had just glanced off had been a totally unexpected land mine. It went up in the moment that his body fell across it. Treffry tamped the explosion, which gutted him like a kipper and blew through his backbone. But a lot of force went downwards and earth flew. If in his last moment Treffry had been capable of thought he would probably have considered his deep feelings about grave-digging to have been justified. In any case, as Hanbury remarked callously, he had at least saved everyone a lot of sweat. The explosion had softened up the ground very nicely indeed and from then on it was fast work. And all three bodies were buried together in the one wide, shallow grave. Cameron hadn't liked putting a Free French underground fighter and a British naval rating in the same grave as a Nazi, nor had anyone else, but this was war and expediency had to rule. The main worry was the racket of the explosion and Cameron was inclined to think they should get back to La Linea by some other route than the road and warn Gomez.

'Much too risky,' Hanbury said. 'Besides, it wasn't all that loud, except to us.'

This was perhaps true; the site was lonely enough, which was why it had been chosen by Pedro Gomez, and so far there had been no reaction to the bang. Hanbury gave it as his opinion that the land mine was pre-war, something left over from a Spanish Army exercise, or even, and perhaps more likely, from the Civil War that had put General Franco in power.

Cameron insisted on one thing: all hands were withdrawn from the shed itself and moved back through the cork oaks for a couple of hundred yards.

But no one came.

By this time the US Task Force, the great battleships behind the security of the anti-submarine screen provided by the destroyer escort, were within five days' steaming of the Gibraltar Strait. They would make their landfall off Cape Trafalgar to the south of Cadiz. The US Admiral aboard the *North Dakota* was poring over the charts for the Mediterranean approaches, and those for the Mediterranean itself, with the officer, a commander, responsible for navigation and with his meteorological officer, a lieutenant JG of the USNR. The weather ahead was expected to become unusually bad for the time of year. Gales were forecast to sweep down from the Bay of Biscay while the Mediterranean itself, though currently seasonal, would go through one of its dirty periods, with a strong wind expected from the east, from the Levant, which was more or less in the area of the forthcoming operations against the Piræus. Times and distances were being meticulously checked and re-checked; Vice-Admiral Rice was a meticulous and conscientious officer, often too much so for his staff's liking.

He drank coffee and stubbed a finger on Cape Trafalgar, just before ending the conference and dismissing his staff to their bunks.

'Cape Trafalgar, Abe,' he said to the commander.

'Yes, Admiral?'

Rice frowned and pushed out an already protuberant lower lip. 'Can be tricky, I guess, in dirty weather. Right?'

The commander looked puzzled. 'Don't reckon on any difficulty, Admiral.'

'Well, no, maybe not . . . maybe not. Just a hunch, Abe. Something I don't like. But maybe I'm seeing ghosts.'

There was a grin in response. 'Nelson, maybe. Battle of Trafalgar, all those wooden walls. All that bull.'

'Ah, come on, now, Abe! It wasn't bull, it was a great fight, you know that?'

'Yes, sir, sure I know that. I was referring to all the bull the limeys have put up since. The limey Navy lives on Nelson, on memories. England expects – you know?' He paused. 'I don't reckon we're going to sail into any ghosts, Admiral, any of Nelson's sail of the line beating hell out – '

'All the same,' Rice interrupted, 'I'll be darn glad when we're clear away through the Strait.'

The Commander caught the met man's eye and gave him a wink behind Rice's back. The Admiral was suffering from what the flagship's wardroom had come to call a bad case of the Brits. He didn't want to balls anything up, anywhere within sight of the British bastion of Gibraltar and the stiff necks of the British Navy. Yet it seemed to go beyond that: the Admiral had appeared definitely uneasy. He had never been the man for hunches, not until now. Apart from a certain old-maidishness, an over-insistence on detail as it seemed to many, he had his feet firmly on the deck. That mention of a hunch, plus ghosts, communicated unease to the Commander, and when he left the cabin he did a re-run of everything, just to be on the safe side. The re-check showed him that all was well; he hadn't been guilty of any navigational cock-ups and the Task Force wasn't going to be piled up on any Cape Trafalgar, nor on Carnera Point, nor on Europa and never mind the weather.

None of them in the approaching Task Force had any idea as to what was going on in Cadiz, into the orbit of which the ships would pass as they made up for Cape Trafalgar. In fact the intention in Cadiz, where the *Kaiserhof* was not far off being in all respects ready for sea, was that the Americans would never reach Cape Trafalgar at all. Captain Rudolf von Arnim, a four-ring Captain of the Imperial German Navy, one of the old sort, trim-bearded, autocratic, a stiff-backed disciplinarian, intended to position his command some one hundred miles due south of Cape St Vincent, right across the track of the Americans as they made their inward leg, launch his midget submarines and at once turn back towards Cadiz. He was confident that most of the submarines would penetrate the destroyer screen and fire off their torpedoes successfully. And that would be that. Von Arnim did not expect any opposition from the British Navy; certain diversionary plans were to be enacted at the right moment, certain false intelligence fed into the grapevine, and the dunderheaded British Fleet would hasten away to the east . . .

A little before another dawn came up over Andalusia the remainder of Party Highwayman came in with Pedro Gomez. One of them was the Chief ERA as promised, by name Trelawney. There was no fresh intelligence, Gomez said, and no change in any of the orders. The guns and ammunition were brought up from the hole in the ground, the shed was left with nothing to give away the fact of its recent occupation, and the party went back down the track to the road, moving silently, carrying the sub-machine-guns, grenades and ammunition. Gomez had told Cameron that their transport was waiting: a bus, such as was seen in plenty on the Spanish roads; if stopped, Hanbury would say that they were a party of workmen being moved from the docks at Malaga to San Fernando on orders from Madrid.

'Here's the documentary authorization,' Gomez said, handing a lengthy form to Hanbury. 'No one's going to question that. It'll get you into the dockyard. After that it's up to you, Cameron.'

Cameron nodded. 'There's the question of concealment of the arms,' he said.

Gomez grinned. 'All taken care of –'

'Somehow I thought it would be!'

'You'll find the bus has a load of sacking and clothing aboard. Have the guns stripped down before you get to Algeciras, and bundle the parts up. It won't be queried – Spanish workmen on the move always carry smelly bundles of personal possessions with them. All right?'

'All right,' Cameron answered. There was a curious sensation in his guts. The time of danger was starting now and it was going to be a danger such as he hadn't experienced before. It was true he had carried out operations ashore, in Crete and in Norway; but in both instances there had been strong anti-Axis groups at work, which meant friendly faces. Here in Spain all was for the Nazis and apart from his own men the last friendly face he might see was that of Pedro Gomez himself, and he had to get back to La Linea.

5

As soon as the ramshackle bus started up along the road to Algeciras Cameron told his CPO to get the guns stripped down and concealed. There were enough for every man, plus revolvers for himself, Hanbury and Penrose. The bus itself was appalling – typically Spanish, full of authenticity and chickens' feathers: it had done its share of taking the peasantry to market along with their livestock and, according to Hanbury, it wouldn't have been cleaned out from one year's end to the next. The driver, Gomez had told Cameron before parting, was a worker on the Marquess of Bute's estate and his Anglophilia could be relied upon absolutely. The Marquess was an excellent landlord and employer and the driver, by name Luis Acebo, had been – and in fact still was although the family had been absent since the start of the war – the Marquess' foreman forester in the cork woods. Cameron spoke to him; he couldn't wait for the British to win the war and for the family to return to Guadacorte. In the meantime, with a cigarette hanging from the corner of his mouth, he drove like a man possessed of the devil. Cameron, fearing as he did for the safety of his party, for the ancient bus was taking it badly and the brakes seemed non-existent, had a word with Hanbury.

Hanbury said, 'Leave him. They all drive this way.'

'Don't they come to grief?'

'Frequently. But a slow Spanish driver would attract suspicion immediately.' Hanbury himself was hanging tight to the seat as the bus lurched round bends almost on two wheels. At one point they just missed an army lorry coming the other way, and fists were brandished between the two drivers, and oaths were hurled at unheeding ears. Cameron made an effort and took his mind off the road, looking left towards Gibraltar Bay and the Rock rising immense and grand beyond. Aboard the ships the day's harbour routine would soon be slipping smoothly into gear: Both Watches, Divisions, Hands to Quarters Clean Guns, Stand Easy, Out Pipes, Up Spirits, Hands to Dinner, Both Watches again, Evening Quarters, Libertymen, Hands to Supper, Rounds and Pipe Down. It never varied, unless Hitler's aircraft intervened, in any of the widely flung parts of an Empire at war . . . in a sense the familiarity of it all held a feeling of home and it was very different from plunging crazily through southern Spain in an unprotected bus. As they approached Algeciras on the side of the bay opposite Gibraltar, Cameron caught glimpses of the Straits beyond Tarifa Point. A heavily-escorted convoy was passing through, probably to Malta. Cameron counted some dozen deep-laden merchant ships including two tankers. There were a couple of big liners, obviously carrying troops. The escort included cruisers and an aircraft-carrier – *Formidable*, according to Hanbury.

It occurred to Cameron that the convoy's destination might be the Piræus rather than Malta. Hanbury, who seemed to know a good deal more about the war's strategy than he himself did, refused, rightly enough Cameron knew, to be drawn. He said, 'We might drop in the shit, you know. If we do, well, then we might be questioned by Nazi agents.'

'I suppose they'd obey the Geneva Convention?'

Hanbury laughed. 'If you believe that, you'll believe anything. Anyway, the less you or your lads know, the better. Just in case.' He added, 'It'll all come clear later – after we've boarded. I know Pedro Gomez spoke of the Piræus – but only because he had to. You had to know the urgency, Commander.'

Cameron waved a hand towards the passing convoy. 'They'll be all right, anyway.'

'Yes. But if we fail, then nothing'll ever pass through so easily again.'

They were now not far off Algeciras.

In the bus behind Cameron one of the men who had joined overnight from La Linea had also looked with longing at the friendly sight of the Rock of Gibraltar. And its Naval hospital. Leading Seaman Leroy had a problem. He was virtually certain he'd picked up what was known in the Navy, when you wished to be polite, as a dose. Leroy was no hanger-back when it came to having a good time ashore, and a good time meant drink and women. The ladies of easy virtue to be found in droves in Devonport, as well as in Pompey and Chatham, Glasgow, Belfast, Londonderry and Rosyth, were mostly not much cop and if he hadn't been as tight as a drum Leroy probably wouldn't have taken the risk. But that was what he had done, just twenty-three days before he'd been detailed by the Drafting Master-at-Arms for Party Highwayman. Only a few hours after being detailed, he'd noticed what he believed to be the first signs and he'd been worried stiff.

It was his duty to report it. If he didn't, and it was later discovered, he would have committed a Naval crime and he could even lose his rate. As a leading hand, he was supposed to be responsible. But his self-diagnosis might have been wrong and if he made anything of it he might be thought to be trying to skulk from the draft. He had gone around with a long face and a pre-occupied manner for the next couple of days and when the signs seemed to lessen he had decided not to report to the Sick Bay and then, lo and behold, it was too late. He was on his way to Gibraltar.

This morning the signs had come back, and come back worse. There was no doubt about it this time. He could now be done under the Contagious Diseases Act, not to mention the bloody Articles of War, he thought in anguish as Gibraltar with the hospital and all its doctors became obscured behind the buildings of Algeciras. And any minute now he would begin the long process of rotting away and he would never make PO . . . much less his ambition of ending his service as Commissioned Boatswain like his old man and his grandfather before him.

If ever he found that Devonport whore again, he would strangle her. If not, he'd bloody go and commit suicide. Life took on a hopeless aspect. He knew the longer you left it, the less the chances of a lasting cure. It could be transmitted to future generations, a bloody *congenital* dose. They'd all had lectures on it from a surgeon lieutenant on joining. It was the most important thing in the Andrew. The very first thing, bar saluting everything that moved, that you were taught about.

What a bloody fool he'd been! Bugger Operation Highwayman. He'd wanted to shine, wanted, of course, the thing to be a resounding success. Now it didn't matter to him any more. Better perhaps to be captured by the dagoes or the Nazis, who would provide medical attention and when he came out of a Spanish internment camp, or a German POW camp, after the war, no one in the UK need ever know. Except perhaps one: a girl in Truro, if she still cared by that time. He would never be really sure the cure was permanent – another risk he wouldn't take. Mabel was pure and innocent, she would never understand anyway . . . God, his mind was in a real bloody whirl. Of course he couldn't marry her; he would have to think up some sort of excuse – like he didn't love her any more. That would be a lie. Leading Seaman Leroy, as the bus moved more slowly through the town streets, was almost in tears, his face, as dark and Cornish as that of Penrose, crumpled like a monkey's.

They were approaching the western outskirts of Algeciras now.

'Nazis,' Hanbury said.

'Where?'

'Those two, on the right, coming up to them now. With a Spanish Army officer.'

Cameron saw them. Even in plain clothes they were unmistakably German. The hair was clipped skull-tight and there was a strut in their walk. The features were the purest Aryan. Each step spoke of the Master Race. They didn't so much as glance at the bus with its load of dockyard workers. Presumably they had other matters to attend to: a report to

Berlin on the composition of the recently passed convoy and the strength of the escort, all vital information. If, as was demonstrably the case, certain cruisers and an aircraft-carrier were on their way into the Med, then they were unavailable elsewhere, which was useful for the German Naval Command to know . . . Cameron wished he had General Franco somewhere within range. That dictator was playing a pretty filthy game, making a pretence of neutrality whilst deliberately endangering British lives and succouring Hitler as hard as he could go. In Cameron's view it was time that situation was brought to an end, time someone in the RAF went mad and took it upon himself to order saturation bombing of Madrid or Cadiz or Barcelona. Bring the whole thing to a head and pave the way for a British landing along the southern Spanish coast.

He said as much to Hanbury. Hanbury didn't comment at first but gave a superior smile as much as to say that simple sailors didn't understand politics or Whitehall-level strategy. But a few moments later Hanbury relaxed and said, 'Good grief, no. We can't afford to stretch our resources that far. Quite impossible. Basically, that's what we're here for – to ensure that neturality's *not* breached too overtly.'

'But just the mere fact we're here and we're taking the ship out –'

'Yes. I know it doesn't add up on the surface, but surely that was explained to you in UK? Once we're out, we're out. The great thing's not to be caught in the act. Neither Franco nor Hitler's going to make too much of it afterwards. Adolf will chew a carpet in private. Neither of them want Spain to come into the war. Franco for obvious reasons, Hitler because he's getting all he wants without having to stiffen Franco with whole divisions of German troops.' Hanbury glanced from the window. 'We're coming clear of Algeciras. First stage over.'

'And no trouble.'

'I didn't expect any. Did you?'

Cameron shrugged. 'I didn't know what to expect.'

'No. You're out of your element, aren't you, Commander.

47

Never mind. It'll not take long to get to San Fernando. As I said before, from then on it's all yours. You're the seaman, you're the fighter. I intend to revert to the role of adviser when called upon.'

Cameron said, 'I'd be lost without you, Hanbury. I don't mind admitting it.'

'We make a pretty good team,' the Special Branch lieutenant said absently. Then, in a lower tone only just audible above the racket of the bus, he asked, 'What did you make of our friend, Commander?'

'Gomez? I – '

'Not Gomez.'

'The military chap in Gibraltar?'

'Not old starch-arse either. That doesn't leave many options, does it?'

Cameron said, 'All right, I've got there.' He frowned. 'An oddity to look at . . . '

'That neck – yes. But go on.'

'I don't really know. The setting was curious. That little church. You don't normally conduct operations from churches.'

Hanbury gave a harsh laugh. 'In this bloody war, you conduct 'em from anywhere. Who'd have thought, once, that the British Prime Minister would conduct a war from an underground room adjoining the Admiralty, or the Chancellor of the German Reich live in a bunker?'

'That's air power – '

'Yes, yes, I know there's a difference. But the church in question has seen it all before in a sense, along with perhaps all other churches of its age. Long before . . . I suppose you didn't notice the crusaders' crosses in the stonework around the west door?'

'Crusaders' crosses?'

'When the local men went to the Crusades, they carved a personal good luck cross on their places of worship. And that church is pre-Conquest, or parts of it are.'

'You've been there yourself?'

Again Hanbury laughed. 'We all have, who work for our

48

friend. An interest in church memorials and so on is good cover. According to him.'

Cameron was silent for a few moments, then said, 'I'm not sure why you asked my opinion of him.'

'Never mind,' Hanbury said. 'It's not important – I just wondered, that's all. He's not everyone's cup of tea. But there's a reason why he came to mind at that particular moment.'

'Oh?'

Hanbury said, 'I happened to spot him in Algeciras.'

As the bus carried on along the route, swaying, horn blaring out whenever a pedestrian was sighted, to send that pedestrian scurrying fast off the track, Cameron pondered what Hanbury had said with apparent nonchalance. He wouldn't say anything more, other than that Mr Cambridge, whom he still didn't mention by name, had been coming out of a church with a priest. Possibly Mr Cambridge's interests extended to Spanish churches – but not in the middle of a war. Or in the middle of Operation Highwayman.

Checking up? Could be, but to do that must hold enormous dangers.

And the man in the centre, the spider sitting in the web, didn't go out into the field. Surely – though Cameron hadn't the experience to judge – that was the one thing that never happened? Mr Cambridge hadn't seemed the sort to be careless or stupid. If he had been, he wouldn't have got to his presumably high position in Intelligence – if that was what he was in, which he must be. Not just the ordinary Foreign Office.

It didn't add up; but it added to Cameron's worries. It could be that something had gone wrong. Even the communications set-up provided by the Polish Army in Conington Hall could have struck a snag. Jamming – the Nazis cottoning-on to something, a leak in security?

The possibilities were in fact endless.

Cameron was convinced something had gone adrift and the operation was in jeopardy. But he could be wrong and he forced himself to believe so until something showed which way the cat was jumping.

The bus was full of the stench of the Spanish cigarettes provided back in the hut in Guadacorte. Most of the seamen and stokers were chain-smoking: nerves were strung-up by now. It wasn't only Cameron who was out of his element. Only Hanbury was taking it all in his stride, not even appearing worried about the curious advent of Mr Cambridge. Chief Petty Officer Penrose was worrying not about forthcoming events but about his wife in Elsworth, close to the command centre of all this, however distant that centre – he hoped – might be from danger. Penrose, as totally unaccustomed to intrigue and cloak-and-dagger as was his officer, was a man of imagination. Wouldn't have been Cornish else, he thought. When cloak-and-dagger came in, you never knew who was safe, *where* was safe. His family might be got at if Hitler got to know what was going on in Spain. That very proximity of Elsworth to Conington and its Polish communications link . . . but his missus, she was only a CPO's wife . . . he was letting his mind run riot, it needed some discipline. You're being a bloody fool, Penrose said to himself, drawing his shoulders back as best he could whilst trying to retain himself in his seat behind Cameron. Spanish drivers, cor, lucky for this one there weren't any British bobbies around.

On the wrong side of the road, the bus negotiated a bend, a sharpish one. Just round it, a big, covered Spanish Army lorry was seen coming the other way. The bus driver swung crazily back to his proper side. But the military vehicle slowed and placed itself across the road ahead and an officer got down from beside the driver.

The bus braked hard. Everything fell about the interior, bodies, concealed weapons in their wrappings, plus all manner of dislodged dirt and debris from former journeys.

They managed – just – to avoid crashing into the army vehicle. The driver looked out, cursing volubly. The Spanish officer strode to the window.

50

He appeared to be asking the purpose of their journey, and their destination. There was a torrent of speech, and much waving of arms took place. Hanbury brought out the authorization, got up and went to the driver's window. He passed the document through. The officer scanned it and was about to hand it back when something happened half-way down the bus. A bundle containing some of the stripped-down weapons, one that hadn't shifted under the sudden hard braking, chose this moment to teeter on the edge of the rack above the seats and fall. It fell with deadly aim, right between Leading Seaman Leroy's legs. It was very heavy, and a gun-muzzle took Leroy in his currently most sensitive part, right on the affected area, which was immensely sore and vulnerable.

Leroy screamed in agony. He couldn't help it; he was beside himself with worry already and this was the last straw, the straw the pain of which confirmed absolutely in his mind that he'd really fallen for it.

'Bloody soddin' 'ell!' he yelled out. 'Oh, *Christ*, me – '

He bit off the last word; but by now it was too late.

6

Penrose was on his feet as the Spanish troops, at a shout from their officer, poured from the back of the lorry.

'Steady, lads,' he called. He turned to Cameron. 'We're blown, sir. I take it we fight back?'

Already the seamen were casting off the wrappings and assembling the weapons. Within some fifteen seconds the bus was surrounded. Cameron said, 'Hold it, Chief. We're in a neutral country, don't forget that.'

'We've got to forget it,' Hanbury said. 'If we don't, the whole thing flops and that ship leaves Cadiz.' Beside the driver, the Spanish officer was waving his arms and shouting; a moment later the driver was seized and dragged bodily from the bus. Hanbury went on in a hard, tight voice as the Spanish officer climbed into the doorway with a revolver pointed, 'Any God's amount of British and Allied seamen and troops are going to die, Commander. You can't let that happen. Right now, the road's clear in both directions. It's now or never. We've got the arms . . . the Spanish have got only old rifles. Are you going to go?'

'Wait a minute,' Cameron said. It was a diabolical decision to have to make. The Spaniards were innocents, even if their Caudillo, General Franco, was not. They were neutrals; the consequences of any hostile act could be catastrophic, could even alter the course of the war and result in more men being killed than might be lost as a result of the sailing of the *Kaiserhof* from San Fernando. This factor was imponderable; and meanwhile the Spanish officer was moving into the bus, giving excited orders. Hanbury turned away for a moment and delved down into the seat where he had been sitting. He straightened quickly; Cameron saw the revolver in his hand. It came up fast, and Hanbury fired. The Spanish officer fell with his head shattered and after that it was pandemonium. And self-preservation. Cameron passed the order to Penrose. From every window the sub-machine-guns opened on the Spanish troops, swinging in arcs, mowing them down. A few rifle shots came back; two of the British party went down. Then the rest were pouring from the bus under Penrose. Penrose had seen what had to be done now: a clean sweep, no survivors, or Operation Highwayman was off. And still the road was free of all other traffic in both directions. The whole thing was so far totally unobserved. The road ran through lonely, desolate country burned brown by the sun. Not even an animal could be seen. Outnumbered in any case, the remaining Spanish hadn't a chance against the quick-firing sub-machine-guns. And the bus driver, who'd broken away and gone flat as soon as he could, was all right.

Covered with sticky sweat and clinging dust, Penrose came up to Cameron. 'That just about does it, sir. What now?'

'Get the bodies aboard the bus,' Cameron said.

'The *bus*, sir?' Penrose stared. So did Hanbury.

Hanbury asked, 'What's the idea?'

'We leave the bus,' Cameron said. 'Or better still, hide it in the trees. All of us re-dress as Spanish soldiers. Then we go on to San Fernando. All right?'

'No,' Hanbury said loudly, his face flushing. 'Not all right. Our authorization refers to dockyard workers, not troops – '

'Never mind the authorization. As troops, we won't need it – troops in an army lorry, with all the proper markings. There's another point, too: as troops, we won't need to hide the guns.'

'This lot,' Hanbury said, waving an arm around, 'didn't have sub-machine-guns. If they had, they wouldn't have been of British Army pattern.'

'We'll worry about that later,' Cameron said crisply. 'We can carry the Spanish rifles and have the rest handy in the lorry. I doubt if the lorry'll be liable to a search. Agree, Hanbury?'

Hanbury gave a slow, reluctant nod. 'Right,' he said. 'It won't. But –'

'It's an order, Hanbury. We play this my way from now. Understood?'

Hanbury glared, hands on hips. 'On your head be it. It's against my advice. You don't change horses in mid-stream. Nor do you change the orders half-way through, not without reference to higher authority.'

'Higher authority's somewhat out of touch,' Cameron said, 'so I'll take it on myself. Now we won't waste any more time. Chief?'

'Sir?'

'Fast as possible. Dress all the dead in the dockyard workers' rig before putting them aboard the bus.'

'Aye, aye, sir.'

Cameron had further words with Hanbury while Penrose raised his voice, ordering the hands to smack it about. At any moment something could come along the road. It was still early and the Spanish were not early risers, but that army lorry had come along.

Cameron asked Hanbury about disposal of the bus. It was the driver who answered. There were bends ahead, about a mile, and some longish drops into a valley. The best way, he said, would be to drive the bus ahead, then push it off the road.

'Right,' Cameron said. He and Hanbury lent a hand with the re-dressing; then Hanbury, as the only Spanish speaker, put on the Spanish officer's uniform. The fit, and the fit of many of the others, was all over the show but it would have to do. They worked fast; as soon as the dead Spaniards were aboard the bus, the driver got back in and drove ahead while Penrose himself got behind the wheel of the army vehicle and turned it back towards Cadiz, then followed up behind the bus with Cameron and Hanbury and the remainder of the men now embarked. The two who had been hit by the rifle-fire were not seriously wounded: no more than nicks and some blood. The troops, probably conscripts, had shown little keenness for a fight and no aptitude for handling rifles.

Ahead of the lorry, the bus ground to a halt on the brink of a minor precipice. The driver was about to jump down when a car's engine was heard from behind the lorry. The car went past, going flat out, scarcely even slowing to take the bends ahead, and vanished. Cameron wiped sweat from his face. God was with them this day. If that car had come along five minutes earlier . . . but it hadn't and that was all that mattered.

As soon as it had vanished, the driver climbed out of the bus, and waved towards the lorry. Cameron ordered his party out. They ran ahead and got round the bus, pushing hard while the driver leaned in from the step and manipulated the steering-wheel. As the front near-side wheel went over the edge he jumped clear, landing in a heap in the roadway. More shoving and the bus, with its load of bodies, toppled. Cameron watched it go, bouncing off the side of the drop. It landed on its roof, shattered, a sight of dereliction. As they watched from above, flame began licking from the engine, and smoke rose.

'Right,' Cameron said. 'All aboard for San Fernando!'

Hanbury had brooded for some while after they had got on the move again. 'Well, it's done now,' he said further along. 'I hope you know what you're doing, that's all.'

'We'll have a better chance,' Cameron repeated.

'To wear the uniform of a neutral whilst in that country – it compounds the felony.'

'Only if you're caught.'

There was a silence; the over-crowded lorry rocked from side to side. The road was still pretty bad, full of potholes and with crumbling edges. There was very little traffic. Hanbury started again. 'That man who yelled out. What are you going to do about him?'

Cameron shrugged. 'Nothing, basically. He'll get a bollocking from my Chief PO. It was a natural enough reaction – when something hard lands on you.'

'He nearly buggered the whole show. In effect, he killed all those troops. Still, I suppose that's war.' Hanbury paused. 'Your change of plan. Our friend, and Gomez, to say nothing of the brass, are expecting us to go in as dockyard workers. This will cause confusion, you know.'

'That's war too,' Cameron said. 'You act as seems proper in changed circumstances. Forget it, Hanbury. We're committed now, as you said. We'll just have to take things as they come.'

Hanbury didn't say any more, just shrugged. Cameron's mind worked on, trying to look ahead, to foresee the difficulties that lay between Party Highwayman and the *Kaiserhof*, now preparing for sea if the intelligence reports were right. That bus. It was going to be found, of course. But it might be some while before anybody worried about a missing bus that was not on a routine schedule, and the wreckage, thanks to the angle of the drop, wouldn't be seen from any casual vehicle passing by. Cameron wasn't too worried; in two days' time they should be away. The trouble might come later, when the diplomatic representations went in and he was called upon to explain matters to the Admiralty and the Foreign Office. But that could wait. Present problems were much more pressing: it would be fatal to enter the docks at San Fernando before the *Kaiserhof* was fully ready for sea. The moment had to be spot on. And what to do in the meantime – dressed as soldiers of the Spanish Army?

Had he, after all, been precipitate? It would have been much easier to have hidden themselves away whilst dressed as ordinary working *hombres*. Soldiers were not so easy to hide.

He mentioned this to Hanbury who said, 'Quite. You've set us a problem.'

'One we have to solve fast.'

'Yes.'

'Any ideas?'

'No. Not yet. They may come.'

'They'd better come fast.' They were not so far off Cadiz now.

'How right you are,' Hanbury said snappishly.

'How about trying to contact our friend, seeing he's in Algeciras?'

'That,' Hanbury said flatly, 'is just the sort of thing you *don't* do. Our university friend . . . if he gets blown, a lot else gets blown too. He's sacrosanct.'

'Sorry,' Cameron said with a grin. 'I didn't realize he was all that close to the Almighty. I suppose that's why we met in a church.'

Hanbury glared.

They came, soon after, into the outskirts of the naval port at the inner end of the narrow isthmus connecting it with Cadiz itself. Cadiz was a very old city, founded by the Phœnicians in 1100 BC; but the old town had been virtually destroyed in 1596, when it had been sacked by Raleigh and consumed by fire. The modern town, itself ageing now, was well laid out, with fine squares and promenades and some outstanding buildings – the two cathedrals, one dating from the year after Raleigh's exploits, the Torre de Vigia, or watch-tower, the church of Santa Catalina containing one of Murillo's master-pieces, the academy of fine arts . . . more importantly Cadiz, well sheltered on the Atlantic side, was a perfect harbour for Spain's peacetime maritime trade with Europe and America. But the great naval station of San Fernando with its shipbuild-ing yards and port facilities was of first importance to Cameron and his party. The naval dockyard would be – it was – well guarded; Cameron's task appeared the harder now he was seeing the extent of the base for himself. It would be difficult enough to board the *Kaiserhof* in the first instance, with his meagre complement of men against five hundred, though far from all that five hundred would be fighting seamen. To get the ship out was going to be an even tougher nut to crack, however lightly Gomez had spoken of it. It was quite a distance by water from San Fernando all the way down the isthmus to pass Cadiz for the open sea . . .

The driver, the loyal Spaniard from the Marquess of Bute's estate, was asking where to take the lorry. Hanbury interpre-ted, and looked at Cameron for an answer. He seemed to be sourly amused.

Cameron said, 'I'm passing the buck. You know San Fernando. I don't.' It was the sort of response that he hated having to give, but he had no alternative. Once again, and fervently, he wished himself back aboard a ship at sea. There, he had no need to dither, to pass any bucks at all. He had a sudden flash of anger against NA2SL and the odd-looking Mr Cambridge. Hanbury wasn't helping; there was an air of I-told-you-so – natural, perhaps. Hanbury was the expert, he should have listened to his advice. But he was still convinced they would have a better chance in Spanish uniforms ultimately. A short period had to be covered and that was all. And they had to be sure of getting intelligence from the dockyard as to the progress of the *Kaiserhof* in making ready for sea. That part, the intelligence, had to be left to Hanbury.

The Special Branch lieutenant said, 'There's only one thing we can do. Leave the lorry here, split up, and make independently for the red-light district. That's where half the naval and military population's likely to be found at any one time – and no questions asked. All right?'

'Two queries. What about the language, and how do we find the red-light district if we can't ask the way?'

Hanbury said, 'As to the language, it'll have to be a case of shut traps and hope for the best –'

'If one goes, we all go. That's not on. We have to stick together. We're all dependent on who speaks Spanish: you and the driver.'

Grudgingly, Hanbury saw the point. The lorry continued into the port's surrounding area of criss-cross streets. Even here the traffic was light; Spain was suffering a petrol shortage, one which even Herr Hitler was unable to make good, having his own uses for all the petrol he could lay his hands on. Hanbury, seeming at a loss, had words with the driver, then looked happier. To Cameron he said, 'He'll drive us right to a farm on the north of the town. Guaranteed safe – old friends of his. It's a long way from the dockyard but it's the best we can do – in the circumstances.'

'Right! It sounds a safer bet than the red-light district

anyway.' He added, 'Just to mention one thing, the lads would have been rooked of – '

Hanbury snorted. 'I never suggested they should become customers. Just that they should mingle . . . just until I'd fixed something up.'

'You have someone who can do that?'

'Yes, of course. It was all arranged, but that's off now. My contact will have to dream up something else.'

'I think this farm will do us very nicely,' Cameron said.

They drove on through the town. The streets were thronged with people, largely walking in the roadway. The shops seemed full of goods – food, wine, clothes, furniture – all the signs of peace, the luck of a people who had been kept out of world conflict. They certainly wouldn't want to lose their neutrality. There were pretty girls occasionally seen, heavily chaperoned by stout mothers or aunts. From near the tailboard, Leading Seaman Leroy looked out, saw the girls, saw them lustfully and with regret. He couldn't go with any girls any more, it wouldn't be right. Might just as well have it shot away and be done with it. These Spanish girls . . . he'd heard it said Spain was still a Victorian country, and they looked more modest than Queen Victoria herself. You'd never be able to get through the chaperone screen, in a special sense the anti-torpedo mob. But it was always the same with women, by and large; the decent ones didn't, and the others gave you a dose, or anyway the risk was always there, like getting the decent ones pregnant which of course was why they didn't do it, much as they all wanted to. And the falling of that gun had really started something: talk about pain! By now it wasn't so much a torpedo as a sharp knife sticking into his groin.

As they came clear of the north-western outskirts Luis Acebo, the driver, spoke to Hanbury. He sounded rattled. To Cameron Hanbury said, 'He thinks we're being followed. A car. He says it's the one that passed us just before we ditched the bus.'

'Tell him to try to throw it off.'

'Not a chance,' Hanbury said. 'We're nearly out of the town.' But he passed the word on. The driver shrugged eloquently and drove on with an eye watching his wing mirror.

'What d'you think it is?' Cameron asked.

'No idea.'

It could be Spanish police in an unmarked car, it could be Nazi agents. Cameron was about to suggest to Hanbury that they might do better to take a side turning and dive back into the town where there would be a better chance of a throw-off when the car came past them at speed and drew well ahead, passing another lorry, a civilian one that seemed about to fall to pieces. Cameron blew out his breath.

'Panic over,' he said.

'I wouldn't be too sure.'

'Why not?'

'It could have gone to the farm.'

Cameron stared. 'Has it got second sight?'

'Not exactly,' Hanbury said. 'But I saw who was in it. Two men. One was a priest. The other . . . remember what we saw, or I did, in Algeciras?'

Once again, a sense of alarm. What was Mr Cambridge doing? Cameron asked, would he be likely to know about the farm?'

'Yes. I would think so. Luis Acebo would have been closely investigated and all his friends and contacts will be known. You don't go into this sort of thing without full preparation. Our friend would have all the facts. Yes, he'd know about the farm. Now he's putting two and two together.'

'Something's gone wrong, then?'

'It begins to look like it,' Hanbury said. 'No use speculating. We'll know soon enough.'

They drove on. It was getting towards midday now. Work had been suspended in the fields. As they came out into the country men and women were resting, eating bread and cheese washed down with the local vino. Waves were exchanged with the supposed soldiers as the lorry passed. The heat was intense, sweltering, and sweat ran freely. It was like being in an oven. Too hot even to think straight . . . Cameron felt as though he was being pressed into the ground by the very heat. The air disturbed by the vehicle's movement was hot and brought no relief at all. The sun struck down with nothing to impede it. Even in the canvas-covered back, it must be hell for the ratings – worse than for those in the cab, what with the close-packed bodies. The lorry's metal was too hot to touch, but somehow the engine was coping with it and the radiator didn't appear to be reaching boiling-point, which was something of a miracle, Cameron thought.

They drove for around one and a half hours, then turned off to the right of the road and along a track similar to the one by Guadacorte. Olive trees grew alongside, and here and there eucalyptus. The track was a long one, and climbed towards its end. As they came clear of the olive groves Cameron saw farm buildings and, away to the south and west, the deep blue of the sea beyond the port of Cadiz. There was no sign of a car.

'This is it,' Luis Acebo said in Spanish to Hanbury. They all piled out. From a door in the farmhouse a man and a woman came out, wizened people in their sixties, very dark-skinned, smiling and deferential. Hanbury spoke to them, a longish conversation, then he turned to Cameron. 'Two old retainers of the Marquess of Bute,' he said. 'Married while in the noble service. Only too anxious to help. They disapprove of what El Caudillo is doing against Britain. 'The Marquess,' he added, 'gave them this small-holding. His generosity's rubbing off on us. Like the French of old, they regard all Englishmen as milords. Any minute now the old lady's going to curtsey.'

She didn't, quite; but Cameron recognized the enormous respect. And the courage: General Franco wouldn't be easy on those of his subjects who went against his edict and the old couple stood to lose their property and perhaps their lives if anything should leak. The risk they were taking was enormous. Cameron shook their hands and smiled; he couldn't communicate with them, but asked Hanbury to convey his gratitude and admiration.

They went inside, Cameron and Hanbury bending their tall

61

bodies as they went through the doorway. It led straight into a living-room with shuttered windows. It was remarkably cool after the terrible heat outside. They sat, and vino was brought in an earthenware jug. Cameron asked about Penrose and the hands. Hanbury spoke to the old man. They would be accommodated in his barn and made very comfortable. The British party could stay as long as they wished and they would be safe. The couple had three sons, who would be watching. Immediate warning would be given if anyone approached, something that the old man didn't consider likely. He had no contact other than on market days with the world beyond his property. The couple were wholly self-contained and self-supporting.

'But if someone does come?' Cameron asked.

Hanbury said, 'The lorry's going to be hidden under a bloody great pile of straw. As for us, we scatter – the old chap's told me where. He says we'll hide up easily . . . and no worry about tyre marks or footprints, not on this ground.'

It was like iron. You could drive a tank over it and it might not show. But Cameron was immensely uneasy now: despite all the assurances there was danger in the mere fact of the lorry's presence. If there was any delay now, its absence from wherever it was supposed to be was going to be noted and there would be a search. Better if they had been able to leave it deserted in a San Fernando street – or would it? Its very desertion would have raised queries and alarm. But there was going to be alarm soon in any case. That alarm might extend by natural process of suspicion to the future movements and safety of the *Kaiserhof* and her lethal brood, and the guard would be reinforced to the point where no one could ever have a hope of getting through.

And Mr Cambridge?

Hanbury hadn't made any mention of him, no questions to the old couple. He could have been mistaken about the occupants of that overtaking car, though this was unlikely, taking into account Mr Cambridge's odd appearance and the companionship of the priest. If he wasn't here, where was he? Why had he gone on past? The answer to that was probably discretion: cars that follow on lonely roads stand out like sore thumbs, and not only, perhaps to those being followed; and Mr Cambridge certainly wouldn't want to be the object of any attention.

In the coding room of Flag Officer Gibraltar a signal in Naval cypher was being broken down into plain language by a paymaster lieutenant. When decyphered it was taken at once to the Chief of Staff, who brought it to the attention of the Flag Officer in person.

'Originated by PA1, sir.' This was the call-sign of the Polish communications HQ at Conington Hall. 'Passed to Admiralty, thence to us. Prefix Most Immediate and Most Secret, as you can see–'

'Yes. I see all right.' Rear-Admiral Evans read the message. It told him that intelligence collated by the Poles in Cambridgeshire gave cause to believe that the *Kaiserhof* was moving out ahead of schedule. And that Mr Cambridge had apparently moved out of Emmanuel College, whereabouts not currently known. In short, he'd disappeared.

Evans said, 'Prepare a signal immediately, ask Admiralty to report movements of Mr Cambridge as soon as known – *someone* must have the information. They need a prod. As to the *Kaiserhof* . . . ' He drummed his fingers on his desk, absently.

'Yes, sir?'

'I don't know . . . I suspect the Nazis and their Spanish friends may have been putting out false information earlier – about the state of the ship's readiness. Just in case we picked it up. Make us think we had more time if we were intending doing anything about it. This early movement – totally opposite to what we've been working on. We've got to move fast, Renshaw.'

'Cameron and Hanbury, sir?'

The Flag Officer nodded. 'God knows how we tell them! They're out of communication. To try to infiltrate a messenger at this stage could be risky, put the whole thing in jeopardy if he was bowled out.'

'I agree, sir.' Captain Renshaw looked worried. 'Another thing: the chain'll be out of operation now the whole of Party Highwayman's gone through. Gomez won't be expecting another bod, he'll have nothing ready – '

'Yes.' Evans stood up. 'Spanners in the works – never a good thing when one's coming up to zero hour. Hanbury's got his contacts in San Fernando and Cadiz, after all, and they'll have been keeping their eyes open. I think we have to leave it, Renshaw. Leave it to Cameron, the man on the spot. But I'd like to know what's happened to that Intelligence bugger – Cambridge. Admiralty's obviously worried or it wouldn't have been passed on to us here.'

7

The response to the Chief of Staff's signal came back to Flag Officer Gibraltar a couple of hours later, after further contact had been made with the Conington Hall communications HQ. It was now known that Mr Cambridge had reported to RAF Wyton near Huntingdon, had produced high level authorization and demanded to be flown out for Northern Ireland. The station commander hadn't queried the request – the Foreign Office was good enough and he knew Mr Cambridge personally. Nothing further was known as to Mr Cambridge's movements after the aircraft had touched down at an airfield south of Belfast but if anything came in it would be reported. There was something about the signal that worried Evans: there was a hint of something not having been said, of a veil being drawn. Damn secrecy!

He didn't like it. He was being kept in the dark. People didn't suddenly vanish in Northern Ireland – unless it was over the border into the Irish Republic. But why should Mr Cambridge do that?

At the farm north of Cadiz, at about the same time as the Flag Officer was pondering over Mr Cambridge, one of the old couple's sons came in at the rush: a car was coming up the track from the main road. There was no time for an evacuation. Cameron looked through the slats of the shutters. As the car stopped, Mr Cambridge got out, with his attendant black-clad priest. The farmer went to the door; there was a conversation in Spanish, a lot of it, according to Hanbury, a reverent greeting to the priest. Then the farmer

65

came back with the two of them and Mr Cambridge came forward and shook Cameron by the hand.

'You're surprised to see me, no doubt, Cameron.'

'Very, sir. The last thing I expected – '

'Yes, I know.' Mr Cambridge's head wobbled on the long, thin neck. 'It's not something I normally do. But the matter was very urgent. I wouldn't have come out otherwise, naturally.' He paused. 'How have things been going with you and Hanbury?'

'All well so far.'

'I'm so glad, very relieved.' Mr Cambridge took out a large white linen handkerchief and mopped sweat from his face. The priest in his heavy black must have been like a furnace. 'Nice and cool in here, but by Jove it's devilish outside, isn't it? Well now, you'll want some detail, Cameron, and you, Hanbury. Glad to meet you both again, by the way, and still alive. I've never underestimated the dangers you've been facing. And still face. My thoughts have been with you.'

'Thank you,' Cameron said.

'There's been a delay. Such a nuisance and it could be dangerous. You're going to have to spend rather longer in hiding than was originally intended. I'm very sorry.'

'What sort of delay?' Hanbury asked.

'The objective. You know what I mean – I don't like too much precision. Not ready yet, not ready to move. Trouble, I believe, with the – the motive power. You understand? If you went in as planned, you'd be caught like rats in a trap. For certain, that is. Even if you took the objective – which we expect you would have done, of course, so I shouldn't have used the words *even if* – well, you'd have been stuck there. You'd have been overwhelmed and the whole thing would have come out. That was why I had to warn you.'

Cameron nodded. He asked, 'How long will the delay be?'

'We don't know yet. I gather several days.'

Hanbury said heavily, 'By which time the US Task Force will have moved through into safety. Good news – of course. But I'm very surprised the Nazis aren't pulling their fingers out a bloody sight harder to be ready in time.'

66

Mr Cambridge had raised his eyebrows. 'You know about the Task Force?'

'Yes. Told in Gibraltar. Sorry – not in Gibraltar. By Pedro Gomez, in La Linea.'

'I see. Well, as you say, it's good news for us, isn't it? More so for the Americans. As for the Nazis, they'll have other targets. But I don't see why we should worry about them, other than to stop their little game.'

'I'm not worried about them,' Hanbury said. 'Just surprised that all that German expertise and technology can't get her away on time – that's all. Did you,' he added, *'have* to come out yourself, sir?'

'Yes. You'll not expect me to be precise, but there were and are good reasons why I was forced to come into the field. It wouldn't have been my own choice. I've not even been able to warn Gibraltar, I'm sorry to say. Technical difficulties at PA1 . . . they're inundated with radio traffic between there and their own units and some of their equipment's on the blink. There was no time to get authorization to switch the communication link to the FO or Admiralty. You know how these things are. Or perhaps you don't.' Mr Cambridge mopped at his face. 'It's all frustration, especially when Churchill gets a new bee in his bonnet and switches his interest.'

It didn't quite add up, didn't wholly convince. Too much unexplained, especially in regard to the use of radio. Hanbury asked, 'How did you get in? Into Spain, I mean. From what you've just said, I take it it wasn't through Gibraltar?'

'No, no. I knew of – other ways. Father O'Flanagan – he's Irish of course – met me at a certain place on – '

'That's the truth,' the priest said, beaming. 'Glad to help. I got caught up in Spain when the war started, d'you see, and I decided to stay with me flock and help out if ever the chance came, d'you know?'

'Yes, I see,' Hanbury said. His face had a baffled look. He glanced at Cameron, then away again. He said to Mr Cambridge, 'You certainly took a risk. We're all grateful for that. But I don't like the idea of hanging around here and putting decent folk in danger . . .'

Later that day as the evening shadows lengthened, passing quickly into full dark, no one seemed to know where Lieutenant Hanbury was. Cameron had seen him last, saying he was going for a word with the Naval party in the barn. When Cameron checked with Penrose and Leading Seaman Warlock, they hadn't seen him – he had never been near them. Mr Cambridge seemed curiously upset, wobbling his head more than ever in his evident agitation.

'Where can he have gone?' he asked.

Cameron suggested Hanbury may have slipped away into San Fernando.

'That's a long way on foot.'

'He might get a lift. He has contacts there, sir.'

'Yes, I know. So foolish! He could be in danger, and that pre-supposes danger to the operation. He should have checked with me first. I don't know what we're going to do about this.'

'Nothing we can do. Just wait for him to come back, that's all. If he doesn't come back we'll have to shift our plans, just in case.'

'Shift our plans?'

'Move out of here. For the old people's sake if nothing else.'

Mr Cambridge paced the living-room, went outside, stared down the track, into the olive groves, towards distant Cadiz. He was clearly very concerned; Cameron was no less so. But there was a distinct unease about Mr Cambridge that seemed to go beyond an anxiety that Hanbury might be in danger. There was a vengeful look in his eye, a distraction in his manner as he turned back from his scrutiny of their surroundings. He said, 'You spoke of moving. We mustn't do that whatever happens.'

'We can't put that old couple in danger, sir.'

Mr Cambridge waved his arms. 'They're not important. Oh, I know what you mean, of course, and it does you credit, Cameron. But the stakes are so high.'

68

'High for them too.'

'Yes, yes. But they knew what they were doing, they were willing to accept the risk.'

Cameron frowned. 'All right, let's forget them for a moment. If there's a risk to them, there's a parallel risk for us, isn't there? A risk to Highwayman. Doesn't it make sense to move on, and hide up somewhere else?'

'I don't know yet. I really don't. We must wait to see what Hanbury's done. There's just one thing, Cameron.'

'Yes?'

'I'm in charge now. I have full authority as you know. I shall give the orders.' He went back into the farmhouse.

Cameron remained outside, thinking, feeling more than ever a sense of danger, of something imminent. Like Cambridge earlier, he looked down towards Cadiz. The area was a blaze of light, with what looked like floodlights over the naval dockyard at San Fernando. Work proceeding on the *Kaiserhof*? It was the devil's luck that the German ship had struck engine trouble. The essence of this operation was to have been speed. Every moment of delay worked against them. Unless intelligence of the delay had reached Gibraltar, there would soon be concern that he, Cameron, had not sent his movement signal. How long the Flag Officer would hold on to things was just one of the imponderables. He might go into some sort of action, precipitate action. There was a desperate need of cruisers to escort the Mediterranean convoys; two such ships could not be held alongside the mole in Gibraltar indefinitely, waiting for Cameron. Operation Highwayman was far from being the only concern of the Admiralty. Earlier, Cameron had asked Mr Cambridge the question direct: why had he not come into Spain via Gibraltar, as the Naval party had? In Algeciras, he'd been close enough to the Rock. Why take another route? Mr Cambridge had clammed up. Modes of entry, he had said, were not for discussion, and he had his reasons for choosing his own route. Cameron had been left to ponder that one. He couldn't help seeing some sense in not using Gibraltar. There were known to be Nazis in La Linea and Cambridge was a big fish. And, as the military man in Gibraltar had said, both the Spanish and the Germans in residence knew very well that there was a two-way traffic through the *aduana*.

Before leaving the farm, Hanbury had shifted out of his Spanish uniform and was dressed as a farm worker, a simple peasant. He had found dirty brown corduroys and a washed-out blue denim shirt in one of the farm's outbuildings. Thus differently incognito, he had slid through the trees as the darkness had started to come down and had reached the road. Walking towards San Fernando, he had picked up a lift aboard a ramshackle lorry that appeared to be tied together with string and smelled appallingly of farm manure. The driver was a sociable sort of chap and talked all the way, though much of his conversation was lost in the din from the engine and the constant rattle of wood and metal from the bodywork. He drove as fast and as badly as any other Spaniard, hands off the wheel for much of the time as he gesticulated. He was an ardent Fascist, a keen supporter of General Franco, and he preferred the Germans to the British. Yes, there were many Germans in Cadiz and San Fernando, the dockyard was full of German technicians, so he had heard, and there was a ship in the naval port, according to rumour, that was soon to go out to sea and spread havoc among the British ships that came impertinently close to Spain to enter the Mediterranean, which by rights belonged, not of course to El Caudillo, but to his great ally Signor Mussolini.

'Of course,' Hanbury agreed. 'But when is this ship to go to sea, have you heard that?'

The answer was, very soon now. And God speed the day, said the driver fervently. He had been brought up on lurid tales of past British wickedness, of Drake and Raleigh and the singeing of Spanish kings' beards and the terrible fate of the Great Armada at British hands. The King of England was the devil incarnate, sworn enemy of His Holiness the Pope – had not his ancestor thrown out the Roman Catholic church, lock, stock and barrel, and burned down the monasteries and killed the monks and abbots, and then attacked the convents and raped the nuns? If the present king of England had the chance, he would do the same all over again. It failed to tally with George VI, but Hanbury kept his tongue in his cheek and agreed. He was put down a short distance from the naval dockyard and as the lorry drove off the driver waved and shouted loudly, '*Viva Franco*!'

Hanbury responded with an equally loud, '*Arriba España*!' which, whilst perfectly acceptable to the Spanish people, was not quite so forthcoming. A rigid arm was extended from the driver's cab and Hanbury responded to this too, but as his arm came down again all but two of his fingers were curled away.

He walked towards the dockyard. By now it was full dark and floodlights had been switched on. There was the sound of rivetting hammers at work, and other shipyard sounds. It was as though Spain was at war. Such night-time activity was seldom heard in a country at peace, and the noise spoke loud and clear of work going on upon the *Kaiserhof*. The Nazis would be prodding hard, anxious to get the ship away to sea and her deadly work.

Hanbury didn't linger near the dockyard; it was too risky.

Turning away, he walked back along the way he had come and then, going off to his right, he plunged into a maze of side streets and narrow alleys. Here were the dwellings of the dockyard and merchant shipyard workmen, small houses poorly furnished and smelling at this hour of preparations for the evening meal, smells of fish, of *pælla*, of omelettes of various kinds.

Hanbury stopped at a door and knocked. Two taps, then a pause, then two more. After a short interval the door was opened by a young girl dressed in black. She greeted Hanbury with a smile and pulled the door wide. He went into a room at the back, where a fat man was sitting in vest and braces, reading a newspaper. As Hanbury entered, this man dropped his paper and got to his feet, smiling a welcome.

'Ah, señor, so long since you have come, and in such good time for a meal –'

'Sorry, Felipe. I can't stay.' Hanbury paused. 'Are you on

holiday, or something? The yard's still at work – '

'Si, señor, it is at work and I am on the night shift. There is much work, so much work to be done, there is no time for holidays until – '

'Until the German has left port?'

The fat man nodded, his unshaven jowls wobbling like a jelly. Hanbury said, 'A little bird tells me there has been a delay, Felipe. Engine trouble. How's the work going – what's the new time of departure?'

'That is a secret, señor. I myself . . . I work on the *Kaiserhof* but I am not told these things.'

'Perhaps not. But you keep your eyes and ears open. You always do. And you must have seen the state of readiness for yourself.'

A shadow had passed across the fat man's face. 'There is much danger from the Germans, señor.'

'Yet you're a brave man, Felipe. You fought against Franco, didn't you?'

'This must not be mentioned – '

'Nor will it be again. You remember Barcelona, you remember the bloody fighting, you remember the Alcazar. I needn't remind you.' Hanbury said no more, but he was recollecting many things. He himself had been caught up in the Civil War, had fought against Franco in the International Brigade. The fighting had been intense and bitter, the bloodshed had been appalling, the cruelty of Franco terrible. He knew that Felipe Urquijo, now known as Felipe Bella, would be remembering other things: how, by order of El Caudillo himself, his father and mother had been garrotted in public, his wife and his two sisters pierced to death by the bayonets of Franco's German troops, having first been raped many times. He would be remembering that the Englishman, Hanbury, had saved his life by slaughtering a whole infantry platoon of Nazis, and then spiriting him away to the south, through much danger. Felipe had changed his identity once he was in Andalusia, and had survived the Franco purges. And he still worked whenever he could against El Caudillo, the murderer of women and children . . .

72

Felipe was staring into the distance, not seeing the close confines of the little room, not seeing his daughter standing in the doorway. He was remembering.

Taking a deep breath he said, 'Señor, there has been delay, yes. This has been overcome, the trouble put right. I do not know for certain, you understand . . . but I believe the *Kaiserhof* leaves Cadiz at first light tomorrow morning.'

Startling news: a tic started in Hanbury's face as he stared at the Spaniard almost in disbelief. 'Loaded with her midget submarines?'

Felipe nodded.

Hanbury blew out his breath. The US Task Force would not be far off, was now once again at risk. The time was desperately short now, he had to get back as fast as possible to the farm. This news from Felipe was a complete turn-around; the *Kaiserhof* was suddenly ahead of schedule – not behind time as Cambridge had said. Felipe could be wrong; as he had said, such as he were not told the facts, they were simply urged on to work faster. Hanbury asked him again; he was sure, he said. He had picked things up. He had no doubt in his mind at all. Hanbury, on a sudden impulse, said, 'You told me you were on the night shift. Would it appeal to you to leave Spain, Felipe? That was what you wanted years ago, I remember.'

Felipe's eyes lit up with sudden wonder. 'Señor, it is what I dream of, to go perhaps to Gibraltar where I can be both Spanish and British. But I have never crossed the frontier because of the risk. My real identity – '

'Yes, I understand that, Felipe. I'm giving you the chance. If you'll help . . . later tonight, when I return . . . then I'll offer you a passage in the *Kaiserhof* and see that you're transferred to a ship that will take you to Gibraltar. I can't go into more detail for now. But it'll come very clear before the dawn. Well?'

Felipe hesitated, his jowls wobbling more than ever, his eyes still alight but now with anxiety in them. 'Señor, there is my Maria, my daughter – '

'Yes. Tell me, Felipe – does she ever go into the dockyard?'

Felipe nodded. 'Often. When we are on long shifts, with no breaks allowed the last few days, the wives and daughters bring coffee and cheese – '

'Then let her bring you some tonight, Felipe. She'll go with you. You have my word on that. And not a word to anyone outside this room, you understand?'

Ninety minutes later, once again having been lucky with a lift, Hanbury was walking up the track to the farm, going fast. One of the farmer's sons was on watch and heard him coming. He came out from the olive grove, holding a shotgun.

'Halt! Who is that?'

'A friend,' Hanbury answered. 'British. I think you understand.' He had his revolver out and was ready to shoot first if he had to.

A torch was flicked on, played over Hanbury. 'Walk ahead of me to the house,' the farmer's son ordered. Hanbury moved past him and carried on towards the house. There was a light burning in the living-room. Hanbury went in ahead of the gun. Cameron and Mr Cambridge were there. When Hanbury was identified, the son left the room and went back to his watch.

Cambridge said, 'Well, really! I'm glad to see you back, I must say, but – '

'There's no time for talking,' Hanbury said. 'I've been in San Fernando . . . with an old comrade-in-arms. He's to be trusted – absolutely.' He paused, staring at Cambridge. 'Your intelligence was wrong, I'm afraid. The *Kaiserhof* leaves at first light tomorrow. Or that's what's intended. We have to get there first. All right, Mr Cambridge?'

Cambridge was licking at his lips, eyes narrowed. A pulse beat in a knotted vein in his forehead. He said, 'I don't understand. I'm not sure I believe you.'

'You've got to believe me, Mr Cambridge.' Hanbury turned to Cameron. 'I'm asking you to believe me too,' he said. 'You're the officer in charge. I'm asking you to give the order to move out at once. Well?'

Cameron said, 'Consider it given, Hanbury.'

74

'Thank you. One more thing. I don't know what Mr Cambridge's intentions are, but I know what ours should be. Mr Cambridge must come with us. Somehow, I prefer not to lose sight of him from now on.'

8

Cambridge was indignant when Cameron confirmed the order; he did so in full reliance on Hanbury, who must be presumed to have his reasons. Hanbury was no fool; and Cameron had already had some doubtful thoughts about Mr Cambridge.

Cambridge said, 'Now look here, both of you. You're working for me, not the other way round. It's ridiculous to suggest I should go with you! It's just not done. Control must be from the outside. What are your reasons for this?'

Hanbury's mouth was a thin line. He said, 'Your intelligence hasn't been too good, has it? If we'd relied on you, we'd have been too late. But perhaps that was the idea.'

Cambridge went red. 'Are you suggesting I'm a traitor?'

'Not necessarily,' Hanbury said. 'I'm just asking Cameron to take precautions in case you are, all right?'

Cambridge looked dangerous but said nothing further. Within the next half minute the Chief PO had been alerted and was turning out the hands. Luis Acebo, the bus driver, dislodged the straw from the army lorry and brought it out. There would be enough petrol, he said, to reach San Fernando. He himself was to leave the lorry in the outskirts of the naval port and make his own way back to La Linea; one of the disguised Naval party would take the lorry on to the dockyard. The priest, Father O'Flanagan, had already driven away in his car earlier in the afternoon; Cameron now regretted having let him go, though in all truth he could scarcely have detained him. He might prove dangerous if Hanbury's view on Cambridge should turn out to be correct,

76

but there was nothing to be gained by worrying about it now. Hanbury was concerned that the army lorry would have been reported missing and the hunt would be on, but he agreed with Cameron that this was a risk they had to take. Without the transport, they couldn't reach San Fernando in time. Briefly Cameron spoke to the hands, outlining his tactics. 'It sounds as though there's a rush job to get the ship away,' he said. 'That means she won't be ready, fully ready, until just before departure.' There was always a last-minute panic at the best of times, after any refit or any period in dockyard hands, long or short. 'That being so, we may have to keep the brakes on for a while once we're in the area. It's no use boarding and then finding we can't take her out. That's suicide all round.'

'So what do we do?' Hanbury asked. 'Hang about outside the dockyard, and attract attention?'

'Not outside the dockyard. *Inside* it.'

'God Almighty!'

'It's logical. We can't take the risk involved in loafing around the streets, and we must be on the spot in case she is in fact ready for sea. Also, there's a risk involved in a last-minute bash through the gates. Another thing: they just may close all the dockyard gates for a while before the *Kaiserhof* leaves – we can't take a chance that they won't. It would be the sort of precaution I'd expect in the circumstances. So we go in right away on arrival. As the officer, Hanbury, you tell the gate guard we've been ordered in to supplement security –'

'And if he doesn't believe me?'

'It'll be your job to make bloody certain he does. You've got a convincing manner –'

'Thanks! It's not always guaranteed to work. Anyway – suppose they let us in and then check back?'

'If that happens,' Cameron said, 'we board right away and take a chance on the state of readiness.'

'It's full of loopholes,' Hanbury said angrily.

'So is everything in this sort of war. If you have any better idea, I'll listen to it.'

Hanbury hadn't; Cameron continued with his briefing. Once alongside the German ship, all the supposed Spanish soldiers would be turned out and fallen in – all except Leading Seaman Leroy and one able seaman, who would remain hidden in the back of the lorry with sub-machine-guns covering the *Kaiserhof*'s decks. The moment Cameron gave the order, if he had to, the German would be under raking fire while the main body of men ran for the lorry to bring out all the weapons, ammunition and grenades and then stormed the gangway. Once aboard, Cameron would make a dash for the bridge. Penrose, once all was secured below, would report to the bridge and take the wheel for the run out past Cadiz to the open sea. The leading telegraphist would locate the w/t room and stand by to make the departure signal to Gibraltar. The Chief ERA and his party of armed stokers would fight their way below and take over the engine-room. It sounded, Cameron said, pretty hopeless; but it didn't have to be. Very few of the German ship's company would in fact be carrying weapons. No more than the gangway sentry and perhaps one or two others. The ratings knew this to be true: aboard a ship, no one carried arms. It wasn't like the army, each man with his personal rifle. Aboard a British warship, all rifles were secured with chains running through the trigger-guards, padlocked to the racks under the charge of the keyboard sentry. And it took time to issue them. There would be more than a little panic when the British broke cover.

Fifteen minutes after Hanbury's return the party was on the move down the track, with Cameron and Hanbury in the cab with the driver, and Mr Cambridge crammed into the covered body of the lorry with the naval ratings. He would be very well watched; and was now dressed in Hanbury's cast-off farm worker's rig, in which he would pass muster as a simple *hombre* if they were stopped. Cameron, as they drove uncomfortably towards San Fernando, was acutely aware that, if he and Hanbury turned out to be wrong, Mr Cambridge could make life very unpleasant afterwards. As for Hanbury, he was keeping his head down somewhat. He had told Cameron about Felipe and his promise to him; but as yet he hadn't mentioned the daughter. He believed Cameron wasn't going to be pleased about assurances given in his name and there was something about Cameron that said he could be awkward when he wanted to be. Better by far to present Maria as a *fait accompli*.

Further word had reached Flag Officer Gibraltar from the Admiralty in regard to Mr Cambridge. Cambridge had indeed, as Rear-Admiral Evans had already suspected, crossed the Irish border and had turned up in Dublin, making contact with another British agent who had made clandestine arrangements for Cambridge to fly out in a private aircraft, rather dangerously in view of the various warning radar screens, for the northern tip of Spain near Santander. That was as far as news of Mr Cambridge went. But there was concern at the Admiralty and Foreign Office. The man in Dublin had seen no reason to check back with Whitehall – not until word reached him that no one in the UK knew what Mr Cambridge was doing or where he was.

Military Intelligence had then taken a hand.

Cambridge's rooms in Emmanuel were entered and turned over, as was an office allocated to him in a section of the Ministry of Agriculture, Fisheries and Food, of all unlikely places – more cover. Mr Cambridge had had more than one personality. Nothing of interest had been found. Mr Cambridge's past, his antecedents, his contacts and connections were naturally known and he was as pure as snow. An excellent record, quite unblemished, and a man of intellect and loyalty.

Evans' reaction was more down-to-earth. He said to his Chief of Staff, 'Bloody man's either a lunatic or a double agent. I've often wondered whose side the intelligence services are on. It looks like cock-ups all round.' He was about to make some reference to matters in San Fernando when the paymaster lieutenant brought in another broken-down cypher, also from the Admiralty. It read: PA1 *out of communication.* FO *reports no information ex Cadiz.*

'The Nazis have probably liquidated our agents,' Evans

said. He glanced at the clock. 'Time's running short, Renshaw.'

'Yes, sir. Do you want the cruisers ordered out?'

Evans frowned. 'I think not yet. They've not far to go and I don't want them hanging about off Cadiz longer than absolutely necessary. Just their presence alone would give the game away.'

Aboard the lorry, drivers had been changed as agreed, and Luis Acebo had left them. The dockyard gates were ahead now. In line with their Spanish identity the speed was kept up right to the end. The lorry pulled up with a screech of tyres and brakes, alongside a guardroom. Civil Guards and naval personnel were present, acting none too lively in Penrose's opinion as he looked ahead, swinging head and shoulders out from the tailboard. Lousy lot, some of them smoking fags, some minus caps, what a shower. Still, on this occasion he didn't at all object to slackness and inefficiency. He heard Lieutenant Hanbury shouting at the guard commander in Spanish, sounding hectoring. It seemed to work. Within half a minute the lorry was on the move again, lurching over cobbles, picking its way between the usual clutter and muck of any dockyard, only much more so, Penrose noted, in bloody Spain.

Well, they were inside. Action any minute now and none too soon for Penrose. There had been too much time for thinking, so far, and it didn't do. Thoughts led to doubts. And the Lord knew this whole ruddy thing was doubtful enough already. That was what Penrose had felt all along, anyway; but now that they were actually inside San Fernando dockyard it was different. He knew they had a chance. Bullshit, as they said in the Andrew, baffles brains. Sheer audacity had been known to win before now; it was a Nelson speciality, was audacity.

Basically, they had all just to be careful not to talk where they could be overheard. That Leroy! Penrose had had a word with him, quiet but firm, pointing out what a bloody little twit he'd been. 'Couldn't 'ave hurt that much anyway,'

80

he'd said unkindly.

'You just don't know, Chief,' Leroy had said. There had been passion in his voice. Penrose had gone on to say that he'd made so much racket it was as though he had a dose . . . Penrose had turned away then, to see to something else, and he hadn't seen the sudden deep rush of blood to Leroy's face, so he hadn't guessed how right he'd been by accident, and he still didn't know. But he hoped fervently Leroy wouldn't yell out again, not with them all inside Franco's Number One arsenal.

About a hundred yards inside the lorry slowed and Penrose heard Lieutenant Hanbury speaking Spanish again – asking the way to where the *Kaiserhof* was berthed, maybe. In fact Penrose had seen what he took to be the German ship, under a blaze of floods, soon after coming down towards the gate, but of course in a dockyard you could never drive, or even walk, straight towards your objective. There were docks and railway lines and basins, warehouses and stores and magazines, boatyards, ropewalks and whatnot, all of them in the way.

Ten minutes later they stopped, this time apparently finally. There was another Spanish shout from the cab, and Hanbury jumped down with Cameron. Penrose, taking his cue, told the lads, *sotto voce*, 'You 'eard, jump down and fall in.'

They did so. Now they were alongside the *Kaiserhof*. She was a fine-looking ship, Penrose noted, around twenty thousand tons, three islands – the central island having three decks below the navigating bridge – two masts with goal-post derricks. There were six-inch guns fore and aft and close-range weapons on monkey's island above the bridge. Being in dockyard hands she was dirty and her decks were littered with landlubbers, dockyard workmen. Well, they'd all be gone by the time Cameron took the ship to sea, and it wouldn't be long before he, Penrose, had her decks hosed and squeegeed down . . . he pulled himself up short. That wasn't what he was here for, not this time. It didn't matter how scruffy a Nazi ship was, the main thing was to get her back to UK.

It shouldn't take long. Not with British cruisers coming out of Gib, full ahead on all engines.

Chief Petty Officer Penrose, dressed as a Spanish sergeant, took up his position in front of the two lines of ratings and waited for orders.

He watched as a Spanish naval officer came down the *Kaiserhof*'s after ladder and approached Lieutenant Hanbury. There was some voluble Spanish; all smiles with it. They seemed to be getting on together all right and after the exchange the naval officer went back aboard and Hanbury went casually up to Cameron, who was standing apart from the others, a spare hand keeping an apparent workman company – that Mr Cambridge, funny neck and all. Penrose didn't hear what was said but there seemed to be some concern in the air, he fancied. When Hanbury turned away again and began pacing the dockside, stepping carefully clear of bar-taut steel-wire hawsers turned-up around the shore bollards, Cameron, still keeping Mr Cambridge with him, moved towards Penrose and spoke in no more than a whisper.

He said, 'The naval officer asked if the army had got its lorry back. Mr Hanbury didn't know a thing about it, of course.'

'Course not, sir,' Penrose agreed solemnly.

'I think the Spaniard was being funny at the army's expense. But pass it on . . . we're on stand-by from now.'

'Yessir.' Penrose almost saluted, but caught himself up in time. Lieutenant-Commander Cameron, he wasn't the officer now, not in his Spanish rig. Penrose asked in a whisper, 'See the stern, did you, sir?'

'Yes. Odd look for what was once a liner – a lot of work's been done. It'll be to do with the launch mechanism.'

Penrose nodded and Cameron moved away again. That lorry: the moment some bright boy spotted the number and military markings, he just might tick over. But as he'd reflected earlier, brazenness paid off more often than not. He sent up a heartfelt prayer for speed. His professional eye told him that all was ready along the *Kaiserhof*'s decks. The shoreside workers were being mustered, ready for disembarkation by the look of it, and there was a party of Jerries on the fo'c'sle, more of them aft, all set to heave in the wire hawsers when the shore gang cast them off from the bollards. The bridge was manned: Penrose caught sight of a Jerry seaman's cap with its ribbons dangling down behind. There was steam twisting idly round the syren, smoke coming from the single funnel, and there was the vibrancy and hum of a ship with steam nearly at full pressure. Penrose glanced to his left as he heard light footsteps approaching from the direction of the dockyard gate. He saw a girl, no more than about seventeen by the look of her. Dark and pretty, slim, nice figure, dressed in black with a black thing like a shawl over her head. She was carrying a basket in one hand, a jug in the other.

From a chink in the canvas cover of the lorry, Leading Seaman Leroy also saw her. A nice bit of skirt, he reckoned, very nice. Gloom descended: nice bits of skirt would always from now on cause depression. Never mind imminent action, imminent danger, the sight of that girl concentrated his mind on his personal problem.

The girl took no notice of the apparent Spanish soldiers but went straight to the gangway and climbed to the embarkation deck. There was a German naval rating at the head of the gangway, holding a ·98K carbine. He seemed to know the girl. There was a conversation and the girl seemed to be arguing. The gangway sentry grew impatient and pushed her back down the treads. Both Leroy and Penrose saw that she was in tears as she stumbled back to the dockside, white-faced and trembling in the light from the floods.

Hanbury saw her as well, and began worrying. It was by now obvious that the ship was about to move out and the dockyard workers would be leaving any minute. No need any more for food and drink. The girl was too late. Felipe would be distracted, his exit from Spain blocked if he couldn't get his daughter aboard with him – he would never leave her behind. Hanbury glanced sideways at Mr Cambridge, who had also been watching the girl. The man was really nervy now, licking at his lips and darting glances everywhere. As if seeking escape? Maybe, maybe not. It would be obvious to him that things were going to start up any moment now and perhaps a show of nerves on that account was not to be wondered at. Cambridge wasn't a fighter and until now had kept himself strictly in the background. When the bullets began to fly, he was going to be right there in the foreground, quite a change. *Was* he playing a dirty game? Hanbury believed he was, but doubted if Cameron was convinced. Cameron hadn't his, Hanbury's, experience of dirt, the sort of dirt that had abounded in the Spanish Civil War for instance. Cameron would find it hard to believe, really believe, that any Briton could turn out to be a traitor in the middle of a world war. But there had been William Joyce, Lord Haw-Haw, asking the world in ominous tones from his cosy billet in Berlin, 'Where is the *Ark Royal*?' He was still there, making a fool of himself. A lot of the ground had been cut from under his feet when at last the old *Ark* really had gone down.

Still fallen in, standing easy, the hands waited. Each and every one was edgy, with loose stomachs. Why – if they had been accepted at their face value – were not orders being issued to them from the ship, why were they not being made some use of? They were supposed to have come to back up security. Fat lot of use – they would have thought – just loafing about on the dockside. But Spaniards were weird, like all foreigners, unpredictable.

Leading Seaman Leroy in the lorry, as the minutes ticked past and sod all happened, reflected on wogs and dagoes. A sudden thought came to him of a wog in Singapore when he had been there in the old light cruiser *Caledon* before the war. That man had been quite a sight. He was a stevedore of a sort, one of a gang who brought wardroom stores aboard, fresh food and booze for the officers. The man had suffered from elephantiasis of the penis and used to wheel it in front of him on a barrow, looking like a giant pumpkin . . . laid slap on top of the officers' vegetables.

From his chink Leroy watched as Lieutenant-Commander Cameron walked up on the other side of the civvy. Leroy fancied he and Mr Hanbury looked like a guard on the bloke.

Meanwhile something was going on aboard the ship. Orders were being broadcast over the tannoy and more Spanish workmen were coming up from below, crowding along the embarkation deck and around the head of the shore gangway. More Jerries were beginning to appear on deck as well, none of them armed: they looked like an unberthing party.

Zero hour – must be. Leroy stiffened, grasped the sub-machine-gun hard. He heard the heavy breathing of his mate, Able Seaman Kitto, close beside him.

There was tension outside now. All hands and the civvy were looking green in the floodlights. Cameron and Hanbury were staring towards the head of the gangway, where a fat Spaniard had appeared alongside the German sentry and was engaged in vociferous argument and pointing down to the dockside. The girl, calling something out, started up the gangway again.

The sentry stepped forward and aimed his rifle at her. The fat man seemed to go berserk, flailing his arms, knocking the German aside, trying to get a foot on the head of the gangway. Then a harsh voice came from the bridge. A brass hat, four gold stripes on the shoulder-straps of a white uniform – the Captain. Cameron didn't wait any longer. He shouted out to Leading Seaman Leroy, who reacted immediately, looking through the small tear in the canvas. They all had their orders: the Spaniards were not to be hit, the bridge and upper deck were to be given a wide spread of fire, the floods were to be doused.

Bullet ripped out through the canvas, causing panic. Leroy had taken the bridge as his point of aim, Able Seaman Kitto had aimed at the floods. They went out. Under cover of the contrasting thick darkness – the only illumination now left was from the *Kaiserhof*'s gangway light – the rest of the British boarding–party made a dash for the lorry. Penrose, jumping in, dragged out the sub-machine-guns and the boxes of ammunition. Leroy and an AB took charge of the grenades. The Germans were taken, as hoped, utterly by surprise. Bullets sang across towards them, vicious bees buzzing around the bridge and the open decks, bringing down the

German gunners as they ran to the close-range weapons. Already blood was dripping down from the boat deck. Then in the gangway light Cameron saw something that sickened him: the German sentry brought up his rifle and discharged it point blank at the girl, who seemed rivetted to the gangway, scared by the firing. Her body fell from the ladder, down into the scummy water between ship and shore. There was a keening scream from the fat man. He got an iron grip round the sentry, lifted him bodily and dropped him over the side. The man fell, yelling, turned a somersault and split his head open on the stone of the dockside below. At the same moment the *Kaiserhof*'s syren blared out, warning the whole area, a tremendous burst of din as a full head of steam blasted through and hot droplets of water came down on the men along the dock.

From the gates came the sound of vehicles on the move.

9

Mr Cambridge, ashen-faced, was with Cameron as the latter led the boarding-party up the gangway. Hanbury was just behind. Cameron's revolver blazed, emptying into a crowd of Germans running up from aft. The Spanish workmen were impeding more Germans trying to fight through from for'ard, in fact, more than impeding them. The girl's murder had been seen by them all, and they all knew she was Felipe Bella's daughter. Their passionate blood was aroused, and many of them had no love for Germans at the best of times; not all Spaniards were Fascists. Fists smashed into German faces and a number of the ship's company were, like the sentry, lifted and flung over the side. In the meantime the sub-machine-guns, rapid firers, were carrying all before them. Never mind the five hundred Nazis: of those who appeared on deck, none lived for more than seconds. As each head came through the hatchways it was ripped into by intense fire. The result was that after the first couple or so minutes, the hatches remained closed. Above them, dead men lay everywhere in pools of blood. There was a drifting stench of gunsmoke.

Cameron ran for the navigating bridge. As he reached it and found the bodies of the Captain and two of his officers, with the body of the quartermaster hanging over the wheel behind the shattered glass screens, the transport from the gates screamed to a halt alongside and troops poured out. From monkey's island now, Hanbury could be heard, ordering the ship's deserted close-range weapons to be manned by the boarding-party and the barrels turned on the new arrivals.

He shouted down, 'We have you covered. One shot from the dock and I'll open on you.' His Spanish was well understood; the troops look uncertain. Hanbury was still wearing the uniform of a Spanish officer. They didn't want to die in any case. Herr Hitler didn't mean all that much to them. And there was another factor: the Spanish workmen were calling down in high excitement and anger. The Germans had killed a young girl, daughter of one of their own number. The feeling was nasty. In full control of the gangway from his position behind the close-range weapons, Hanbury shouted down to the workmen to get ashore while the going was good, for their own safety. They poured down the ladder, Felipe Bella among them, his face working, tears running. His spirit was broken. He would want to be with his daughter's body. Hanbury, looking down, forced it from his mind. There was much yet to do and there was no time for brooding. War was war, and very nasty.

As soon as he could do so Penrose joined Cameron on the bridge. With him came Leading Seaman Warlock. Cameron went to the starboard side of the bridge and out into the wing, keeping his head low, beneath the cover provided by the wood of the screen. On reaching the extremity he peered cautiously over. There was pandemonium on the dock wall, German officers were now present and seething up and down in frustration as the Spanish argued, still reluctant to fight with the barrels of the close-range weapons, and some of the sub-machine-guns, pointing straight into them. Cameron decided to cause a little more panic, and try to clear away the opposition before he sent his men right out into the open to cast off the wires holding the *Kaiserhof* alongside. He shouted up to monkey's island.

'Fire a burst over their heads, Hanbury!'

'Aye, aye, sir.' It was the first time Hanbury had used the 'sir.' The guns cracked out, stuttering away, firing close. A Spanish cap flew into the air. The soldiers broke ranks, running like fiends out of hell and shouting. Two of the German officers were bowled flat.

'So far, so good,' Cameron said to Penrose, who had come out of the wheelhouse behind him. 'What's it like below?'

'Going our way, sir. The Jerries aren't showing themselves.'

'They will in time,' Cameron said. 'Warlock – identify the engine-room telephone, ring the starting platform. If the Chief ERA's there, tell him I'm starting to move off the moment he has steam, all right?'

'Aye, aye, sir.' Leading Seaman Warlock went off, back into the wheelhouse. He came out again within half a minute. 'Chief ERA's taken over, sir, with Stoker PO Tremain and his two leading hands. Stoker PO Talland's in the boiler-room. Chief ERA didn't have no trouble, sir.'

'Good! And steam?'

'Steam ready to be put through, sir, and the Chief's standing by telegraphs.'

'Right! Get below and take charge of unberthing, Warlock. Single up to the backspring, headrope and sternrope. As soon as you hear the engines turn over, cast off head and sternropes without further orders. I'll come astern on the backspring and as soon as I move ahead, cast that off as well – you'll have to let them all run back into the water, letting them go from inboard. Understood?'

Warlock grinned. 'Yessir! No shore labour available today to cast off from the shore bollards!' He went down the port ladder at the rush. Cameron heard him yelling out for some hands to stand by the wires. He went into the wheelhouse and wrenched over the handles of the engine-room telegraphs, putting them on Stand By Main Engines. Looking through the fore screen he saw Warlock with another rating, taking the turns of the back-up hawsers off the bitts to let them slide back like huge snakes to the dockside. Once again Penrose was beside him. As the back-up wires were seen to slack off aft as well, Cameron said, 'Right, Chief. Slow astern main engines.'

'Aye, aye, sir.' Penrose went to the telegraphs. Within a few moments the ship began to vibrate. The unberthing parties fore and aft let go the last lines, leaving only the backspring. As the *Kaiserhof* moved astern, slowly, ponderously, the heavy backspring, leading for'ard from aft, held her and, acting as a lever, forced her bows off the jetty so that she was pointing away from the side. Cameron passed the next order. 'Stop main engines.' Then almost immediately, 'Slow ahead main engines, wheel amidships.' As the ship moved ahead, the backspring slackened up and was cast off inboard to drop back into the water. At the wheel now, Penrose, said, 'Talk about panic, sir! Jerry and Spanish both. All shout and no do, I reckon.'

Cameron said, 'They wouldn't have been expecting us, Chief. No plan in existence to counter such goings-on as a cutting-out operation by the British Navy!

'No, sir. Buggers shocked into wetting their drawers just about sums it up, sir.' As the kerfuffle broke out beneath the *Kaiserhof*'s counter the ship began to shudder to the turn and thrust of the shafts.

'Half ahead,' Cameron said.

They moved out for the north-north-westerly passage to Cadiz, the land-locked passage, the really tricky part in the close waters inside the barrier provided by the isthmus. At last the firing started from the dock. Bullets flew, bouncing off the steel of the superstructure and the massive hull. The British party kept its collective head down. The Spanish were being very brave now. Cameron identified the telephone to the w/t room and called Leading Telegraphist Bolus. He said, 'Make the signal, Bolus. Grinling Gibbons – that's all, remember.'

'Yes, sir,' came the leading telegraphist's voice. 'I was just about to call you, sir. The transmitter's on the blink –'

'What's up with it for God's sake?'

'Well, I don't know yet, sir. Can't get no power through, that's all I can say at the moment.'

Through set teeth Cameron said. 'Fast as you can make it, Bolus! No signal, no cruisers. And no steaming-party.'

Below on the starting platform, Chief Engine-Room Artificer Trelawney held a sub-machine-gun in one hand, a wad of

90

cotton-waste in the other. Talk about bloody short-handed, but it couldn't be helped. He was in fact getting some forced assistance from the Jerries, but it couldn't be relied on and they had to be watched closely right the way through. Trelawney would fire to kill the moment he had to, and he reckoned they'd hoisted that in right enough. Two of them spoke a little English and he'd passed the word that his first shot would be by way of a warning; it would do no more than take off the balls of the first Jerry to try anything. After that, they could watch out for their lives. Trelawney was a big man, hefty, and had a rock-hard face. No one had ever been known to doubt that he meant everything he said. No reason why Jerries should be the first. He left the starting platform with an armed stoker to guard it and walked in amongst the Jerries, letting them see him close, letting them get the feel of his determination as it were, his determination to do his part in getting the *Kaiserhof* out into the protection of the British cruisers and then the long haul home. It wasn't going to be easy, and it was going to be very long indeed, since Lieutenant-Commander Cameron would no doubt be told to steer a course well to the westward – moving due west from the Straits and not turning north, and then north-east, until they were well clear, or as clear as they could ever be, of the U-boats and the German attack aircraft based in occupied France.

Lousy buggers. Chief ERA Trelawney moved among them, fixing them with hard stares, letting them know he detested their very guts and couldn't wait to open fire.

He was called back to the starting-platform: telephone from the bridge, the skipper on the line. 'All well, Chief?'

'Yes, sir. No trouble.'

'Will it stay that way?'

'Oh yes, I reckon so, sir.'

'Good! We're starting to move down past the isthmus now. 'I'll keep you informed.'

'Thank you, sir.'

Cameron rang off.

In Gibraltar the Flag Officer was reading a broken-down cypher from the Admiralty. This read: *Intelligence reports indicate enemy activity in the northern sector of the Adriatic. Italian cruiser squadron believed left Ancona. Vice-Admiral Malta fully stretched. You are to intercept. Illustrious, Sheffield and Nigeria to leave soonest possible.*

Evans looked up. 'God damn and blast!' he said savagely. He spoke to the Chief of Staff. 'No message from Cadiz yet?'

'No, sir –'

'*Sheffield* and *Nigeria* are detailed for Cadiz.'

'Yes.'

'No destroyers at the pens . . . ' The Flag Officer pondered anxiously. 'I can't drop Cameron's party in it whatever the Admiralty says, Renshaw. Make a signal back to the buggers: ask them for positive confirmation of orders bearing in mind my pre-arranged commitment to the ship coming out of Cadiz. All right?'

The Chief of Staff nodded.

'The point's to be made that Lieutenant-Commander Cameron's dependent on my sending an escort – there's the availability of the steaming-party to be considered too. Without them, Cameron's virtually deprived of an effective ship's company.' Evans paused. 'However, in the meantime *Illustrious, Sheffield* and *Nigeria* are to be warned of possible new orders.'

They waited; an anxious, nail-biting time for Rear-Admiral Evans. Within the hour the confirmation came back from Whitehall: Flag Officer Gibraltar was to obey the last order; the new Italian threat had priority unless the signal from Cadiz had been received in the meantime, in which case the German prize could still be met and brought into Gibraltar instead of a home port, and immediately upon their return the cruisers would proceed eastwards at maximum speed.

By the time that second Admiralty message had been received there had still been no signal from the *Kaiserhof*. Evans could do nothing but despatch the ships into the Adriatic. Thus – though the Flag Officer had no means of knowing it – was the scene set by the Germam Naval Command, through its mendacious overseas intelligence network, to ensure that the United States Task Force should steam without British naval cover into the midget submarines released from the *Kaiserhof*. Only, as matters had turned out, the faked report of activity in the Adriatic was now acting not against the Task Force so much as against the operation off Cadiz. Which, to the Germans, was doubtless just as helpful . . .

There was still no life in the German transmitter. The story was an unfortunate one, but not unique aboard ships emerging from a dockyard refit. What happened in dockyards the world over was a very sore point with the men who had to take the ships to sea afterwards. The Spanish workers had made a dog's dinner of the radio equipment, transmitter and receiver both. In the course of the extensive work done on the ship whilst in San Fernando, something, somewhere had been wrongly connected up – or that was what Leading Telegraphist Bolus believed. And he was stumped to pin-point the precise spot, the precise trouble.

He reported again to the bridge. Cameron asked, 'No reaction from it at all?'

'No, sir. I'll be doing me best, sir. But it could be a long job.'

Cameron nodded and concentrated on his ship-handling, keeping well to the far side of the channel from the isthmus. First things first. And first of all he had to get the *Kaiserhof* out into open water. God knew how he was going to survive afterwards, if there was no protective force waiting. The Germans weren't going to let them get away with it, that was for sure. If there were no cruisers, he would have to vary his orders and turn east for Gibraltar and hope to make Gibraltar Bay before he was sunk. There wouldn't be any hope of reaching UK unescorted.

The *Kaiserhof* moved on, still at half speed. The navigation was tricky; Cameron had no experience of the waters inshore of Cadiz and he wouldn't risk full speed – not just yet. In the

93

meantime the only firing came from light weapons – useless rifles and equally useless automatic fire out of range from along the narrow isthmus. The Spaniards had presumably to show their Nazi colleagues that they were doing their best, but their best was pretty awful and Cameron imagined the German officers on the verge of apoplexy as they watched it.

He conned the ship on. Obeying the stream of helm orders, all of them small ones, Chief Petty Officer Penrose handled the wheel with expert precision. Whatever the fireworks that might yet come, he was relieved to be back at sea. The journeys in the Spanish lorry, not to mention the bus, had been terrible, all that heat, and the fumes . . . and the barn back at the farm had been grim as well. Penrose believed he would never stop scratching. Talk about bugs, the place had been alive. Leroy had spent the whole time rasping at his crutch, which must surely be raw by now, like he himself was under the armpits and beneath the waistband of his rotten Spanish trousers. Never mind, though. Soon he might even get a bath if he was lucky, and then back to Devonport for another draft, when he could get into his uniform with the three brass buttons on each cuff, and be a proper CPO again. In future they could stuff this sort of lark . . . though he wouldn't mind serving under Lieutenant-Commander Cameron again. For an RNVR, Penrose thought, Cameron was a good lad. No hanging back when the action had started. Penrose admired officers who led their men from the front rather than the rear.

'Starboard five.'

'Starboard five, sir,' Penrose repeated, and moved the wheel. 'Five of starboard wheel on, sir.'

'Steady!'

'Steady, sir.' Penrose read off the heading from the compass card. 'Course, 348, sir.'

'Steer that.'

'Steer 348, sir.' Penrose held the ship as steady as a rock. Soon after, it was back a little to port. Penrose thought Cameron was doing remarkably well; he'd had only a short time to snatch a look at the chart, which had been laid out

94

ready for the Jerries in the chartroom. The *Kaiserhof* slid through the dark water, lit now by the moon. Lights were springing up along the isthmus, and there was the sound of heavy transport. Guns being brought up?

Time would tell, and just a moment later it did. There was a sharp crack and a flash of orange-coloured light from the port side. A shell from a light field-gun whined over the fo'c'sle.

Cameron said, 'Shot across the bows in the traditional manner.'

'Which we disregard, I take it, sir?' Penrose asked.

'Of course!' Cameron brought up a pair of German binoculars and studied the waters ahead. He fancied there was a vessel, a small one, standing into the fairway without navigation lights. What it might be hoping to achieve was beyond him. If it stayed where it was, it would be his intention to run it down and never mind its crew, presumably Spanish. At this stage he wasn't going to be held in irons by any considerations of neutrality. From now on the Spaniards would have to take what they'd been asking for so long . . . Just then another shot was fired from the field-gun; they had drawn ahead of it now, and the shell whined down their port side and away into the night. Then the small vessel that Cameron had spotted ahead moved a little out of his track, steering to starboard. Suddenly there was a ripple of fire that seemed to come from something similar to Oerlikons. Tracer arced across the *Kaiserhof*, over the fo'c'sle, over the after decks, over the bridge. After the one burst the firing was suspended for perhaps half a minute; then, when the warning remained unheeded, the guns opened again, tracer swept the decks as before, and as bullets came through the already shattered wheelhouse windows Cameron felt the sting of something ruffling his hair. He ducked, kept his head low. The fire was maintained, making pilotage harder and much more hazardous. Hanbury, who had come to the bridge as the field-gun had started up, swore suddenly and swung round holding his left shoulder. Cameron asked, 'How is it?'

'I'll survive.'

'You're not needed up here at the moment. Get below and

dress it. There's bound to be a sick bay of sorts that you can raid.'

'It's all right. Just a graze.'

'It's an order. I don't want to have my only officer incapacitated for want of a bandage . . . to stop the bleeding at least.'

Reluctantly Hanbury went below, using the port-side ladder from the bridge. The firing was still kept up along the starboard side. The object was clear enough: the Spanish, or the Germans, meant to wipe out the British without damaging the ship. It looked as though they could succeed, given time. On the boat deck Hanbury almost fell over two men, both dead. As he examined them he saw that one was Leading Seaman Warlock, the other was an AB named Bonchurch.

Nothing he could do.

Straightening, he went down to the embarkation deck and walked aft, looking for an entry to the superstructure where he might find the sick bay. He was losing a lot of blood and Cameron's order had been a sensible one. But he stopped looking for an entry when he saw a man at the after end of the embarkation deck, moving across, stupidly considering the gunfire from the attacking vessel, from port to starboard.

Cambridge. There was no mistaking that.

Hanbury put on speed and came round the stern and up behind Cambridge. He was padding along softly and what with the noise of the Oerlikon or whatever it was, Cambridge hadn't heard him. Hanbury watched for a moment. Cambridge was not all that visible now, for the deck and superstructure above was obscuring the moon. Hanbury wasn't sure whether or not Cambridge had lifted a hand to the vessel off their starboard beam, but there was a suspicion in his mind. Signalling to the boat, asking, perhaps to be taken off before it was too late? Daft as it might seem, that entered Hanbury's mind as a possible explanation of the man's antic in placing himself where he might be sliced into by the tracer.

He came close up behind Cambridge, thus risking his own life also. Cambridge still hadn't heard his approach. In a conversational tone, Hanbury said. 'Asking for a lift, Mr Cambridge?'

Cambridge swung round as though shot. His mouth came open but at first he didn't utter. Then he said, 'What on earth are you talking about?'

Hanbury shrugged. 'Nothing really. I just thought that perhaps that boat was coming for you, that's all. I expect I was wrong.'

'Yes, I think you were. I don't like your attitude, Hanbury.'

'I'm sorry about that.'

'I think you owe me an explanation.'

'Perhaps I do,' Hanbury said, 'but not here.' The tracer was still coming across and he felt exposed. Cambridge shrugged and moved round to the safer side, followed by Hanbury. As they went they felt an increased vibration from the screws. Cameron was coming up to full speed now and soon would come the time of most danger, the time when they would have to pass the naval dockyard at Cadiz.

As Hanbury and Cambridge reached the safer side Penrose was staring ahead from behind the wheel. On the port bow the lights of Cadiz formed a cluster of menace. The *Kaiserhof* might come under heavy fire from the shore batteries or from Spanish – even German – warships laid across to block their outward passage. So far there was no knowing. All Penrose knew was what Cameron had told him: there was no boom across the harbour entrance like, for instance, the anti-submarine boom that ran across the Clyde from Cloch Point to Dunoon to protect the big-ship anchorage off the Tail o' the Bank opposite Greenock. The Spanish authorities had seen no use for such. They were neutrals, the Axis powers were friendly, the Allied powers would never breach neutality. Like heck, Penrose thought, and gave a hard smile behind Cameron's back. Surprise had worked wonders back in San Fernando, no reason why it shouldn't do something similar off Cadiz. Except – of course – that it wasn't going to be a surprise now. The Spaniards would be ready. Too late to rig a boom, yes, but not too late to intercept. It all depended on how far they were prepared to go: the *Kaiserhof* would be better recaptured intact than sunk, obviously . . . and Penrose was thinking about the German ship's company under hatches. Those Germans were having more or less the whole run of the ship below the main deck, except for the engine spaces and boiler-rooms, the kingdom now ruled over by the Chief ERA. The Jerries could attempt a break-out at an awkward moment; but with luck they wouldn't get far. All the openings to the upper deck were watched and the British ratings would be nicely trigger happy. And once they were away . . . well, Gibraltar, if that was where Cameron decided to take the ship, was no real distance off. Once they got there, it would be nothing more than a disembarkation of Nazis en route for the POW camps in the UK.

Ahead of Penrose Cameron said suddenly, 'There's something coming out now. Port bow.' He moved to the engine-room telephone and called the starting platform. 'Chief – bridge here. Coming up to Cadiz. Stand by for possible bumps. I may have to ram.'

'Aye, aye, sir.' Trelawney replaced the telephone on its hook. He left the starting-platform, had a quiet word with each of his ratings then went into the boiler-room to warn the Stoker PO. Not the Nazis; if those buggers were alerted as to bumps and such-like, they'd be ready to grab their chance. With no fore-knowledge they'd just crash on their arses. Trelawney hoped the skipper would be reasonably selective as to what he rammed. The *Kaiserhof*'s bows would slice nicely enough through something small but if she hit armour plate she would look like the cow with the crumpled horn and she would make far too much water for comfort – or safety. But the skipper could be presumed to know that for himself.

Chief ERA Trelawney went back to the starting-platform, watching dials and gauges with a sharp eye. All was well. And he had a few knots in hand if the skipper wanted them. He rasped a hand across his unshaven cheeks: he was beginning to feel like a Spaniard and all, dirty, almost lousy. Dirt didn't do the morale any good at all, but it might not be for much longer now. Trelawney's thoughts, as he waited for some sort of crunch, flew across the seas to home, which was in Torpoint, just over the Tamar from Devonport. That was where his heart lay, on the fringe of Cornwall, where the missus was. She would be worried stiff. Reporting back after night leave to the barracks in Devonport – only a matter of days before, though it seemed like years now – he'd been presented with his draft chit. Immediate move; and no time to let the missus know anything. One of the regulating petty officers in the Drafting Master-at-Arms' office was a pal of his and had promised to drop in on his missus and reassure her that all was well, but Trelawney knew Alice like the back of his hand after just on twenty-two years of being married to her and he knew she would worry. Most people, not just Alice, worried themselves sick over the unknown, and his pal the crusher wouldn't have been precise – couldn't be.

Trelawney remembered something else, and grinned to himself as he did so: he had a son, twenty years old now, who'd joined the Andrew soon after the start of the war. Billy . . . he'd joined as an ordinary seaman and after training at the shore establishment *Ganges* at Shotley in Suffolk he'd been drafted to Pompey barracks. That had been in the autumn of 1940. There had been a scare – the Nazis were supposed to have landed on the south coast. There had been tales of a battle in the Channel, which was said to be running with blood. A load of codswallop as it turned out, but while the scare was on it was taken seriously. All ratings on night leave in Portsmouth had been rounded up by the Naval patrols and the civil police and ordered to report back to barracks.

Billy had been one of them.

He'd found the parade-ground a sea of ratings milling around, with officers and petty officers yelling and getting themselves and everyone else in a right mix. Eventually, along with hundreds of others, Billy had left Pompey in one of a large number of coaches – Southdown, White Heather, Byngs, all the charas that in peacetime set out on mystery tours and so on from near the South Parade Pier – and had found themselves decanted in a field somewhere near

Fareham, where they had dug trenches and settled down with their rifles, a hundred rounds per man, iron rations, and mess traps dangling all round them from straps attached to their webbing equipment, to wait for the Nazi invasion and repel it.

Billy had been there a fortnight. He'd managed to write home towards the end of that time, posting the letter in Fareham. Having no writing paper, and no money to buy any because the scare had interrupted the fortnightly Pay Office handout, Billy had written, in pencil, on toilet paper.

Alice had been convinced he was in cells as a result of some misdemeanour or escapade; Billy was prone to high spirits, a bit of a tearaway. He'd written when he wasn't supposed to, on the only paper allowed in cells, and had got one of the cell sentries to smuggle it out of barracks and post it. According to Alice, all this was . . . largely because Billy had missed his usual weekly letters home and had been vague about his movements in the toilet-paper one. Careless Talk Costs Lives, and Be Like Dad, Keep Mum . . . he'd been well imbued with all that. Trelawney had been totally unable to quell Alice's anxieties and she'd suffered torments until Billy had come home on leave and put it right.

Daft, but that was Alice. Currently, she would believe her old man to be dead and she wouldn't believe he wasn't until he walked in one fine day and kissed her.

Women!

Trelawney's thoughts were roving on when the telephone whined again and he answered. 'Starting-platform –'

'Stand by, Chief. Hold tight!'

Trelawney grabbed for a hand hold and then there was a monstrous jerk and the whole engine-room shuddered as the way came off sharply. A moment later something clanged against the side plating, a booming sound that filled the engine-room like a tolling bell.

10

Penrose wiped a hand across his sweating face. Cries were coming up from the water: the *Kaiserhof* had sliced right into the Spaniard, a gunboat of some two to three hundred tons. The vessel had broken in half, the stern portion banging its way along the big ship's side until the wreckage fell away astern and sank. Cameron was searching out the next hazard. His engines were still moving full ahead. Two men came to the bridge: Leading Seaman Leroy, and Mr Cambridge. Leroy had used his initiative and had checked round below in the fore part of the ship. He reported no damage, no entry of water. The *Kaiserhof*'s bows had taken it well.

Cameron asked, 'What about the Germans in the foc's'le?'

'Pretty cowed, sir. I went in armed, of course, and a hand with me. I reckon they just don't know how few we are, sir.'

'We'll keep them in ignorance as long as we can,' Cameron said. 'All right, Leroy, thank you. Keep an eye on the fore peak, just in case a seepage develops.'

'Aye, aye, sir.' Leroy went down the ladder. Cameron was approached by Mr Cambridge, who was looking grim.

'I think that was unwise, Commander. To hit that boat.'

'It was necessary. Unless we wanted to hand the ship back.'

'There's going to be no end of a fuss in London.'

Cameron said, 'Those who're going to make it, weren't here when it happened. They weren't faced with the alternative.'

'Still – neutral persons! No, it was most unwise. I must insist on one thing.'

'Well?' Cameron was short; his attention was ahead,

where a searchlight from the dockyard was being swung onto them.

Cambridge said, 'I imagine you'll keep some sort of – of log. I think that would be proper. I wish it to be entered that I did not condone your action.'

'As you wish,' Cameron said. Cambridge hung about, looking uncertain. The beam of the searchlight swung blindingly, right into the bridge. Cambridge put a hand over his eyes until he had turned his back. He blundered about in front of the wheel and met a dirty look from Penrose. Penrose didn't care much for civvies aboard a ship, they were just clutter. Especially those who talked bollocks. Penrose knew Cameron had been right, neutrals or not. Nobody liked doing it, no seamen ever liked leaving other seamen to it and never mind their nationality, but it had been inevitable. The Spaniard had virtually committed suicide, standing right slap across the *Kaiserhof*'s course.

Cambridge seemed mesmerized by Penrose's stare. Like a rabbit in a car's headlights, Penrose thought. Suddenly Cambridge said, 'You. What did you think?'

'Me, sir? Not my job.'

'Not your job to think?'

Penrose answered woodenly. 'You know I didn't mean that, sir. If you want to know . . . I think the Captain was dead right. And maybe I'd better have *that* put in the perishing log an' all.'

'There's no need to be rude.'

Penrose didn't respond. Daft bugger, he thought, doesn't he know there's a war on? To his relief, Cambridge left the bridge, big head teetering on the scraggy neck. By now the searchlight had shifted its aim and was playing along the upper deck. No apparent reason that Penrose could fathom out. He reckoned it was probably just scaring tactics. No one liked being under scrutiny of a searchlight. Then another one came on, this time from over to starboard.

'Another ship,' Cameron said.

'Seems like it, sir.'

'Hold your course, Chief.'

'Aye, aye, sir.' Capable hands kept the *Kaiserhof* dead steady.

'We're not so far off the point now. I'll be turning to port soon.' Cameron lifted his binoculars again. He looked to starboard, towards the ship carrying the searchlight. But the beam moved full on to him and all he saw was light that hurt the eyes. Possibly, he thought, the idea was just to blind the bridge personnel so that they piled up, a better way, perhaps, than risking gun damage. That impression was strengthened when the searchlight began to overtake them and was kept beaming on to the bridge. The vessel carrying it was fast, most probably a destroyer. And it looked as though her intention now could be to move ahead and block the fairway. Cameron didn't believe the *Kaiserhof* would withstand an impact against a destroyer – not without sustaining some damage herself. If she began to make much water and go down by the head, even Gibraltar was going to be out of their likely range. This was going through Cameron's mind when a telephone whined and he moved across to answer it.

It was Leading Telegraphist Bolus. 'Transmitter working, sir.'

Cameron blew out a breath of relief and thankfulness. 'Well done, Bolus! Make to Flag Officer Gibraltar immediately, Grinling Gibbons. There won't be any acknowledgement.'

'Aye, aye, sir. I suggest I make it three times, sir. Just to make sure like.'

'Yes, good idea. We're not exactly going to give away our position however many times we make it!' As the call was cut Cameron saw that the overtaking vessel was now well ahead and drawing to port across his course, right where he would need to make the turn around the end of the isthmus to reach the open sea. For a little while yet, he would hold his present course.

Away to the east in Gibraltar, the Flag Officer received the belated report: the *Kaiserhof* was moving out. It was a bad day for Rear-Admiral Evans. He said, 'No ships available.

Someone at the Admiralty ought to hang. I warned the buggers. Now there's nothing we can do.' He drummed his fingers on his desk, looked out at the lights of Gibraltar, the lights of Algeciras across the bay. It was the very devil to have to let somebody down, somebody who'd been promised vital assistance. It wasn't the way the Navy liked to work; and on a lower level, a much lower level of self interest, it was always the senior officer on the spot who carried the can afterwards. The Admiralty would admit no blame, though it was hard to see how they were going to get out of it this time – but they would find a way.

The Admiral got up and paced the office. Force H – those ships with their escorts were bound east, through to Malta. They couldn't be interfered with. There was a convoy to meet, to cover westwards of the Sicilian Channel. The Sicily-based dive-bombers always did their best to make mincemeat of the convoys, assisted on occasions by the heavy ships of Mussolini's surface fleet. There was the US Task Force, coming through from the Naval Operating Base at Norfolk, Virginia – now not far off the Straits. Ask for assistance, for the detachment of some of their escort? That would put the Americans in a spot, unfairly. You couldn't ask an admiral to strip himself of vital cover, and in any case all the US ships were urgently needed further east.

It wasn't on.

Likewise the convoys, passing westwards of the Straits, bound south for the Cape from UK ports, or the other way. The same thing applied – and in any case they would be much too far off to be of immediate assistance. Their cruiser escorts were fast, but not that fast. And currently there was no convoy poised to make the entry of the Straits and the passage eastwards into the Mediterranean. The next was some days' steaming away, well out into the Atlantic and not yet made the turn to port to head inwards for Cape St Vincent.

Dilemma. Worse than that – no options left. Cameron would be out of Cadiz, if he made it at all, within the next hour presumably. From San Fernando to the end of the isthmus was a matter of seven miles, no more. Further, of course, to the open sea and the Straits. Cameron might take it slow, he might take it fast. But an hour must be considered the maximum to Cadiz, and he was much more likely to take it fast, smashing his way through the opposition, the strength of which was itself an imponderable. It would all depend, in Evans' view, on whether or not the Germans themselves had any warships in the port – and the last intelligence reports had made no mention of any. He didn't believe the Spanish would stick their necks out too far. Cameron might yet get away with it on his own, despite the withdrawal of the cruisers. He would have enough sense to disregard the orders to take the *Kaiserhof* to the United Kingdom. Gibraltar was not so far off – and neither the Germans nor the Spanish could be sure there was no escort waiting. In fact they would be bound to assume there was.

'Port ten,' Cameron said.

'Port ten, sir. Ten of port wheel on, sir.' They were in narrow waters now, where the jut of the Spanish coastline bulged out towards the end of the isthmus and the city of Cadiz; but the *Kaiserhof* was still moving at full speed, a little over twenty-two knots. The Spanish vessel was dead ahead as Cameron gave the order: 'Steady!'

'Steady, sir. Course, 195, sir.'

'Steer 196.'

'Steer 196, sir.' Fractionally Penrose moved the wheel and came on to his course, meeting the swing with slight opposite helm as the compass card showed 196 degrees. He reckoned the skipper meant to ram again, and automatically he stiffened, thrusting his foot against the binnacle post in front of him. There was going to be a God Almighty impact at this speed and he thought Cameron had gone round the bend.

Cameron seemed to sense this. Without turning round he said, 'Bluff, Chief. Just bluff. Stand by to put the wheel hard over.'

'Aye, aye, sir.' Penrose licked at his lips: they were dry as dust. Cameron was running it close, *bloody* close. That ship, and it had now been clearly identified as a destroyer, was little more than half a mile ahead. Everything was shaking aboard the *Kaiserhof*, and the wind made by her passage was blowing through the gunfire-shattered glass screens into the wheelhouse. Below in the engine-room, Chief ERA Trelawney was watching the steam pressure, the telegraphs, and the Germans all at the same time. The Germans, he thought, were recovering from the initial shock and could be coming to the point of attempting a counter-attack. This wouldn't be a good moment for a fight to break out, nor would it be a good moment to kill most of his German pressed hands. Working under duress they might be, but they were doing their job and he needed them to go on doing it. Trelawney had an eye on one of the Jerries in particular when the engine-room lurched to a violent alteration of course. The starboard side lifted, the port side went down, Men hung on, feet slithering under them on the greasy metal of the deck. Then the ship steadied on to an even keel, but not for long. She went back the other way. Somehow or other Trelawney misjudged it – in fact his attention had been diverted by the sudden movement of one of the Germans towards Stoker PO Tremain, who had momentarily lost full control of his sub-machine-gun.

Trelawney slipped and fell, flat on his back, and something gave. Sudden pain and he was helpless. The German took his chance.

In the wheelhouse a few moments later Cameron said, 'I think we're in the clear now.'

'Looks like we might be, sir,' Penrose agreed, hope leaping. The skipper's bluff had paid off; the Spaniard had shifted at the last moment, evidently not liking the look of the great steel bows of the *Kaiserhof*. They must have looked from a low-freeboard ship like Ben Nevis on the move, bloody terrifying, much more immediately threatening than General Franco. As the Spaniard had begun to shift out from under, making to port, the skipper had ordered full starboard helm and they'd slid neatly past the destroyer's stern, near enough to capsize her with their wake, almost. Then, as the *Kaiserhof* was brought back to port and steadied, Penrose saw the open water ahead, a lovely sight. The Bay of Cadiz, and then the turn to port to pass Cape Trafalgar and then, if the promised cruisers hadn't shown up, on through the Straits to Gibraltar. Penrose was beginning to believe they were going to get away with it after all, that there wouldn't even be a pursuit into waters so heavily guarded by the British fleet, when something odd and totally unexpected happened.

The engines died.

Cameron turned. 'What the devil!' He moved fast for the engine-room telephone.

No answer.

The Spanish destroyer was turning now, coming up astern of the slowing ship. Her captain, too, would be wondering. To Cameron it was obvious what had happened in the engine-room; and without the availability of power he was helpless, a sitting target, prey for any strong force that decided to board, the situation suddenly and cruelly reversed. He was about to speak to Penrose when something else happened. It could almost have been co-ordinated. There was a short burst of gunfire from the fore well-deck and the able seaman on guard duty, standing on the fore hatch and watching the clipped-down doors into the fo'c'sle where the German seamen were berthed, fell screaming and thrashing his limbs. Cameron had no idea where the firing had come from. Not at first. Then he saw a small, wiry German seaman scrambling out from one of the big bell-mouthed ventilators on the port side of the well-deck, clutching an automatic weapon. Cameron, who had already drawn his revolver, fired immediately. The German moved at that moment and the shot smacked uselessly into the canvas-covered cargo hatch. The German turned, lifted his gun, and sprayed bullets over the bridge. Cameron and Penrose had gone flat. Cameron, seeing the swing of the gun, had yelled a warning to Penrose just in time. When he looked for'ard again, the German was sliding back the clips on the port-side doorway into the fo'c'sle, working fast. Cameron fired; this time he found his target but it was too late. The last clip had come off and the door was opening.

A mass of men came out, carrying rifles. Cameron saw one of his able seamen going for'ard at the run and firing point blank into the rush of men. He accounted for quite a number; but his own number had come up and he stopped in his tracks, arms lifted high, and crashed to the deck.

More and more Germans piled out on deck and started to run aft, climbing the ladders to the bridge, swarming into every part of the ship. It was like an avalanche. A lot of the Nazis were caught in the sub-machine-gun fire and went down bloodily, but it was no use. There was a sudden in-pouring to the bridge from both sides at once. Cameron used his revolver until the chambers were empty. The last he remembered was a big man running for him and bringing the butt of a rifle down on his head.

When Cameron came round he was lying on a steel deck somewhere. The vibration told him the *Kaiserhof* was under way again. His head felt as though it was on fire and he felt sick. Three men, Germans, were looking down at him. One was an armed seaman, the others were naval officers. One wore the stripes of a commander or its equivalent in the German Navy. The other officer, seeing Cameron's eyes open, squatted beside him. In accented English he said, 'You will be all right. I shall attend . . . I am a doctor.'

Everything swung crazily and the sick feeling worsened. The next to speak was the commander. His English was good. He said. 'You have killed many of my seamen, and all of you are dressed as Spaniards. I think I would be entitled to have you shot as spies . . . but you are seamen like myself, and I am a German officer. You will be taken to Germany as prisoners of war.' He paused, staring down at Cameron. 'I have taken over the command of the ship, in the place of my Captain who was killed. Now I carry out my Captain's orders, to attack all enemy shipping. You, who I am told is the officer in charge of the British seamen, will be there with me to watch the launch of my midget submarines. It will be an interesting lesson. *Heil, Hitler!*'

His arm came up. The doctor and the rating responded.

The acting Captain went away with the doctor, leaving the armed seaman to back away behind and go through a watertight door that was at once clipped down. Cameron slid back into unconsciousness. He was not out for long. When he came round again he felt a little easier and realized for the first time that he was not alone. They were all there, those that had survived. Penrose was one of them, so was Hanbury, whose shoulder had been properly bandaged. Trelawney was another; his back, he said, was stiff and and a bit painful still but nothing serious – something had clicked back into place. Stoker PO Tremain, he said, had bought it. Leading Telegraphist Bolus had survived; he spoke to Cameron. He said, 'I managed to get a message away, sir – after which I smashed up the whole caboosh, transmitters, receivers, the lot –'

'Well done, Bolus! The message you sent out – did the Nazis tick over?'

'No sir. No way they could.' Bolus added, 'Had to be in plain language, sir, us not having any code books, but –'

'What did you transmit?'

'The facts, sir. *Kaiserhof* back in bleedin' Nazi hands. I made it to Flag Officer Gibraltar. Don't know if it'll be much help, sir.'

Cameron said, 'It's a warning. I just hope someone passes it on to that US Task Force.' He paused. 'Where's Mr Cambridge? Is he with us?'

It was Hanbury who answered. 'No. He was taken to the Captain's quarters. He's probably selling us for thirty pieces of silver.'

11

The message from the *Kaiserhof* went at once
to the Admiralty for action. In the Operations Room deep in
the fortress-like building beside Horse Guards Parade there
was consternation. Consternation, and an awareness that
something had to be done about it. At least the *Kaiserhof* was
now out in the open and could be attacked. And yet not so.
There was still an insistence from Downing Street that all-out
attack was not desired. The German was still to be taken
intact if possible – and it had to be made possible at all costs.
The least damage the better.

The Duty Captain gave a snort when word of this reached
him. 'There's a certain VIP,' he said, 'and I'll name no names,
who regards miracles as normal daily events. If you ask me, it
simply can't be done, sir.' He was speaking to the Vice-Chief
of Naval Staff.

'Quite! However, it has to be. As you suggested, God has
spoken. I tried to argue, to *reason* if you like. I made the point
that to destroy the damn ship would put paid . . . but no. We
need the know-how. I don't disagree with that, but the price
of *not* attacking her is in my view too high – but that's by the
way, of course. I'm not the PM.'

'So?'

'So we make our dispositions,' the Admiral said, and went
over to a large-scale wall map of the United Kingdom,
marked with pieces of card bearing the names and whereabouts of all major warships and escort groups in the Home
Fleet and the Western Approaches command. The Admiral
studied this in silence, pulling at his jaw and frowning. He

110

said, 'We're damn nearly naked. Almost every ship committed . . . and too many of the others in dockyard hands for boiling-cleaning and repairs. However.' He swung round. '*Madras* and *Lucknow* are to leave the Clyde immediately with their usual escorts under orders to make all possible speed towards Cape St Vincent.'

'*Kaiserhof*'ll head out into the Atlantic, sir. Isn't it a bit of a needle in a haystack?'

The Admiral agreed. 'What else can we do? I'll request assistance from the RAF, of course. No reason why Coastal Command can't stretch itself.'

'But the time factor – '

'Yes. I know! They'll have to take the direct peacetime route . . . even so, they're going to be slowed, with the weather deteriorating in Biscay. There's no chance at all of their being able to intercept the *Kaiserhof* before that US Task Force shows up, obviously.'

'That's what I had in mind, sir. It's due tonight, about 0100 hours.'

'I'm bloody sorry,' the Admiral said.

'They really must be warned now, sir. There's no point in secrecy at this stage.'

Mr Cambridge and the *Kaiserhof*'s political officer, Hauptmann Jahn, a thin man with a perpetual sneer, were speaking German. Cambridge's command of the language was excellent. He said, 'I was in a very difficult position. Very difficult indeed. Who could I trust? That was why I came myself. To Spain, I mean.'

'For what precise purpose? Just to – '

'To abort Operation Highwayman.'

'In which you failed, as we know. The operation was aborted not by you but by our own ship's company.'

'Yes. I can't deny that, Hauptmann – '

'In Berlin, they will not be pleased. I am not pleased also. So many of our men dead! I lay that at your door. If you had not failed . . . if you had passed a message to us in time, there would have been none of this. I think you are a fool. Or worse.'

111

'Worse?'

The Gestapo officer gave a hard laugh. 'Yes, worse. You spoke of whom *you* could or could not trust. How can I trust *you* for certain? To pass a message would have been simple, I think. Why did you not do this – why, I ask, did you not act *in time*?'

'Does it matter now? The ship is in your hands, and you –'

'Yes, this is true. In one sense it does not matter. In another sense it does. We cannot be sure that we can use you again. It is Berlin who must decide, not me, but I shall make my recommendations in the proper quarter. And meanwhile you are in my hands.'

Cambridge sat silent, head wobbling in agitation. He was thoroughly dismayed and a prey to all kinds of fear. Things had turned out very badly. He had never imagined he would end up in German hands. Yet he had done his best to please everybody, himself not excluded naturally, and to maintain all his contacts for future use. This confounded Gestapo man simply didn't understand. Neither had, nor would, Cameron and Hanbury. It was such a very tricky game to play. He waited in trepidation as the Gestapo man got to his feet and went over to a port and stared out at the lightening sea. Cambridge was not *au fait* with current British warship movements, things changed so quickly, but he knew the *Kaiserhof* was in waters extremely dangerous to German ships and he was aware also of the approach of the Task Force from America. The Acting Captain of the *Kaiserhof* would presumably put his midget submarines in the water as soon as possible and then make either back into Cadiz, or perhaps seek some temporary sanctuary in another neutral country – Portugal. The Portuguese were said to be Britain's oldest ally and they had no love for Hitler, but they would provide twenty-four hours harbourage for any belligerent, for what that might be worth. In the meantime the danger persisted and Mr Cambridge remained in his cleft stick.

Hauptmann Jahn turned from the port and gave him his orders. 'You will join the British sailors. You are, after all, a British agent.'

112

'Yes.'

'You will say that you have been questioned, but that of course you revealed nothing. This is understood?'

'Yes, indeed.' The cleft stick, or the noose, tightened. Mr Cambridge was taken under guard to the compartment where the boarding-party had been imprisoned. He was given a cool reception; he had become a pariah. Since he didn't wish the Gestapo to know this, he stopped all comment by placing a finger over his lips, and they took the hint. There would be listening devices; and none of them could be entirely sure of Mr Cambridge's standing. By this time, although the German doctor had not returned to implement his promise of attending to him, Cameron was reasonably fit again. The headache was receding, so was the sick feeling. And there were no bones broken. With Stoker PO Tremain and Leading Seaman Warlock dead, plus eight of his able seamen – and Leading Stoker Treffry in his shallow grave near Guadacorte – he had now fourteen men plus Hanbury, Penrose and – questionably – Cambridge. Not a lot. There was something else, too: the smashing of the W/T, the transmitters and receivers. Bolus had said no one would get that working again short of a dockyard refit. Cameron was in two minds about it; if he managed – it didn't look too likely – to regain control, he would be just as much out of communication as the Nazis.

Cameron, if he were to be honest with himself, saw nothing ahead now but imprisonment for the duration. The compartment they were in was very secure. They were below the waterline; air was entering via the forced-draught system but even so, and even though the compartment was a sizeable one with plenty of room to spare, the atmosphere was stifling and there was an unpleasant fug. There were three electric lights set along the deckhead, behind frosted glass covers. There was no escape from that blazing light other than to shut one's eyes and try to lie on one's stomach. That was all right for some but not for Trelawney, whose stomach was large and uncomfortable to lie on for long, and whose back was being troublesome still. The other alternative was to pull the dirty Spanish shirts over their heads, but then the airlessness grew more unbearable than the light.

Leading Seaman Leroy was taking it badly. Cameron watched him covertly. He seemed to be in some sort of panic – they were all dead worried, naturally, but that was far from panic. Leroy seemed to be muttering to himself, and was neither lying nor sitting; he was walking around aimlessly as though he couldn't keep still, and being a confounded nuisance in the process, disturbing the others with his constant restlessness.

Mildly Cameron said, 'Better save your energy, Leroy.'

'What for, sir? What for, I ask you?'

The voice was tense, brittle.

Cameron said, 'We don't just sit down under this – not right the way through.'

'No hope of getting out, is there?'

'We have to try. That's our duty apart from anything else. Sit down, Leroy. It's the same for all of us, you know.'

Leroy sat and put his head in his hands. His whole body seemed to be shaking. He felt he was at the end of his tether. There was a doctor handy but even if a Nazi would treat him for *that* Leroy saw no way of broaching the subject to Cameron, which he would have to unless he could dream up something else that was innocuous but at the same time urgent. Leroy couldn't bring himself to confess that he'd concealed his condition and had continued to share the same mess traps, or anyway Spanish pots and plates, with all the rest of them. When you reported to the sick bay in the proper fashion and had the thing confirmed, you got shifted from your own mess to the CDA mess, all lepers together, and the mess traps got washed separately from those belonging to other messes, every possible precaution taken. VD made a man an outcast aboard a ship, where everyone was in close contact. Now he'd gone and put them all at risk. He despised himself and felt sorry for himself, both at the same time.

Taking his hands from his face he met the civvy's eye. Cambridge looked away quickly, as though something might be read from his expression. He, too, was scared about something: a fellow-feeling made Leroy recognize that. He

114

doubted if the old bloke had syph, though . . . past that sort of thing. Perhaps it was just his age bothering him. He was old enough to be someone's grandfather, too old to be let loose in peacetime, let alone in the middle of a war . . .

Leroy saw Lieutenant Hanbury get to his feet and go across to sit by Cameron. Hanbury whispered something in Cameron's ear, and Cameron nodded. Leroy couldn't hear what was going on, but a moment later both the officers got up and shifted across to where the civvy was sitting. They sat, one on either side of him. They whispered again, and Cambridge grew very restless, with a funny look in his eye. His voice, when he answered Hanbury, was louder than a whisper, as though he couldn't manage a whisper on account of his agitation. Cameron caught Hanbury's eye, then looked round at the rest of the party. He called to Penrose. 'Chief, how about showing the Nazis we've still got some spirit left?'

Penrose cottoned-on. 'Singing, sir?'

'That's the ticket.'

Penrose got to his feet. 'Right, you heard, all of you. Come on, lads.' He started off by himself; he had quite a good voice. They all joined in one by one. A fairly typical sing-song, as in any Naval canteen ashore. Songs that had been popular just before the war: 'Roll Along Covered Wagon', 'When They Begin the Beguine', 'Down Mexico Way', 'Knees Up Mother Brown'. They forgot about the officers and the civvy, talking together, and certainly no Nazi listening devices would pick up any conversation through the racket. The conversation was a long one; soon the singers had reached the end of the popular tunes and gone into older ones, the 1914–18 war, and Harry Lauder. Then the vulgarity started. Old King Cole featured, so did the King of Rumania, who had a fair daughter, with hair on her dickey-di-do right down to her knees . . . and a lot more.

Cameron had started the ball rolling with Cambridge by saying that an explanation of things past was needed and was going to be forthcoming; and he asked what had transpired when Cambridge had been taken away from the rest of the party.

Cambridge said there were matters he was not at liberty to discuss.

'None of us are at liberty,' Hanbury said before Cameron could speak, 'to do anything. That could be thanks to you. It's now up to you to convince us that it isn't. So start.'

'I really can't say anything. You should know that. If anyone is questioned by –'

'You were questioned?'

Cambridge licked his lips. There was a hunted look about him. He said, 'Yes. Yes, I was. There's a Gestapo man aboard – most German ships have them, there's nothing special about that. I didn't answer his questions, of course.'

'But he knew who you were. If he didn't, he wouldn't have picked on you. There's no need for you to answer that. It's too obvious.'

'Oh no, it isn't,' Cambridge said. 'My age . . . I was clearly not a very likely *active* member of the party, so –'

'So they wanted to find out more about you. All right. I suppose that'd be their line – to explain why you've been sent back to join us, all lilywhite and pure. They're not interested in you any more. Well, I wonder!'

'Do you indeed.'

'Yes,' Hanbury said. 'I do. I believe you're a double agent, Mr Cambridge. Working for us, working for the Nazis. It's nothing unusual. But I don't need to tell you that. The point at issue is, of course, this: whose side are you *really* on? Who's your main employer, where your personal loyalty lies? You'd better sort that one out fairly soon if you ask me. Because sooner or later you're going to have to make a choice as things have turned out. Right?'

There was no answer. Cameron said, 'We have to be able to trust you, Mr Cambridge. You have to trust us too. I see your dilemma. It's a case of the devil and the deep blue sea. But you're going to have to do some talking. One thing among others that bothers me is this: you gave me false information about the time of departure of the *Kaiserhof* from San Fernando. I want to know why.'

Suddenly Cambridge, like Leroy earlier, put his head in his

116

hands. His face seemed bloodless, as though he was in shock. He said, 'All right, I'll tell you. And I'm loyal to Britain, though it may not sound like that to you.'

'Just tell us,' Cameron said.

He did. Complex as the diplomatic moves were – underground rather than diplomatic in the proper sense – it was basically a simple story. Mr Cambridge, already working for intelligence, had been approached before the war, at the time of Munich and Neville Chamberlain's attempt to secure 'peace in our time'. He had been approached by the Nazis because he was known, at Emmanuel, to be anti-Communist and to have friends among Mosley's higher echelons. The British Union of Fascists had appealed to him and for a time he had toyed with the idea of joining them – this was well known in certain Berlin circles. Those circles had never had any inkling, of course, of Cambridge's work for the British intelligence services. On the other hand his Whitehall bosses knew very well his leanings towards Sir Oswald Mosley and he had informed them immediately of the Nazi approaches, which of themselves had given him second thoughts about Mosley. As war had come closer word had filtered through from Germany, whispers of pogroms and of concentration camps filled with Jews, of death by torture, slaughter of women, even of babes in arms. Cambridge had been filled with repugnance. He had retreated rapidly from fascism but had not made his views known to his Berlin contacts. He had been ordered by Whitehall to become a double agent and facilities to this end were accorded him. His reports to the Nazis had been cleverly compiled in conjunction with British Intelligence and although apparently of value never in fact contained anything harmful to the British interest. Cambridge was emphatic on this point. It could all be checked on, he said. On the other side of the coin, he was able to amass a lot of information from the Nazis that had proved remarkably useful to the British war effort – he refused absolutely to elaborate on this now. He was regarded in Whitehall as being extremely useful in his double-agent role and he was expected, because of this, to keep the men in Berlin happy.

Then things had started to go a little wrong; just a little. There were suspicions in the Berlin air and Cambridge had been forced to retrieve his position *vis-à-vis* the Nazis. It had been left to him to do it; it was not a matter in which British Intelligence could be involved other than through himself. That was why he had come personally to Spain.

Hanbury said, 'To bugger up Operation Highwayman, I suppose.'

Cambridge, remembering his conversation with Jahn, flushed. 'That's a harsh way of putting it – '

'But it fits.'

'I suppose in a way it does, yes. But it was vital I delivered – satisfied the Nazis. That was a way of doing it. Giving them something tangible. Can't you understand that?'

'No,' Hanbury said flatly. 'I can't. Highwayman was said to be vital – and I reckon it was. *Is.* It's not finished yet. We're here, and we still have a purpose. Our orders stand even now. So if it was vital, why try to stop it?'

'I've explained – '

'I don't mean that. I mean, do you consider yourself, as a double agent, *more* vital than Operation Highwayman?'

'Yes,' Cambridge said. He didn't say it defiantly or in any sense other than as a quiet statement of fact. He obviously believed it. Hanbury, about to react, held back, frowning. Cameron watched both men closely, looking from one to the other in some puzzlement. He felt that Hanbury was very uncertain now. Then Hanbury asked another question: was Cambridge expecting something to come through from his Nazi contacts, something that he mustn't miss out on, something that was indeed of more importance than Operation Highwayman?

'Yes,' Cambridge said again. 'That's it exactly.'

'Can you tell us what it is?'

Cambridge shook his head. 'I'm afraid not. Not just yet. I repeat what I said earlier, any of us could be questioned and broken down. The less that's known the better.'

'And if you're questioned – properly, I mean, not just as a sort of cover, because they had to be seen to take an interest

118

in an oddball, like this morning?'

'I just have not to break down,' Cambridge answered. 'I don't believe I will, but if it gets bad. . .' He reached into his mouth and brought out his top set of false teeth. Adhering to the plate was a small round phial, about half the size of a man's finger-nail, and another, long in shape but of similar size. 'You crunch them in the teeth,' he said. 'They call them suicide pills. Cyanide. One British and one German.'

Somehow, for absolutely no sensible reason, that seemed to Cameron to establish Cambridge's bona fides.

Later, after a long period during which no one had been near them even to bring food or water, there were footsteps outside, some German conversation, and then the sound of the clips being taken off the door, which was swung open. Four armed seamen under a petty officer were seen and Cameron was identified and ordered out. The petty officer, who had some English, said he was being taken to the bridge. The relief of fresh air was enormous; Cameron took great gulps of it as he came to the open deck. It was afternoon now and the sun was sinking ahead of the ship's course, but was still hot. The sky was brassy, like some huge reflector to increase the effect of the sun. The *Kaiserhof* was cutting a wide swathe through flat blue water, her wake creaming away behind, joined by the curling sea parted by the bows to stream back along the ship's sides. There was a lot of activity starting on the decks fore and aft. Reaching the bridge, Cameron was met by the *Kaiserhof*'s new Captain, the officer in commander's uniform. He told Cameron his name was Schrader. 'I show off my ship,' he said. 'As one who believed he was to be the Captain of the *Kaiserhof*, you will, I think, be interested to see what you have missed.'

'Why bother to show me?' Cameron asked.

Schrader laughed. 'I understand what you mean,' he said. 'The information will be of no use to you until the war is over, when it will be too late – but we Germans, you know, are a civilized race and we treat prisoners according to their rank,

119

and you are an officer who would have had command. You do not object?'

Cameron shook his head. 'No. You said earlier you were going to launch your midget submarines. Is that – '

'Yes. I am all ready. Once launched, they will move in a pack out into the Atlantic. A pack that will savage the American ships that are coming from the west.' There was a strange note in Schrader's voice, a note of almost vibrant pride in what he was about to achieve, which was to be a most glorious feat of arms. Cameron fancied it wasn't so much the act of a civilized race that had brought the vanquished enemy to the viewing platform, as it were, as the result of a desire to indulge in a splendid gloat. The Master Race always went for that.

Schrader spoke again. 'You will be surprised at the speed of launching, Commander. I think it will surprise you very, very much. But you will see.' Schrader, the sun glinting from the gold of the stripes on his shoulder-straps, took Cameron by the arm and propelled him out on to the starboard wing of the bridge. 'Soon, if you look towards my stern, you will see what I mean.' He paused. 'You will not have seen much of the ship below decks, I think. You will have been brought straight up from your accommodation by way of the ladders and hatchways that by-pass the launch deck, yes?'

Cameron said, 'I've no doubt you're right. You know your ship. And certainly I saw nothing that seems likely to be called a launch deck.'

'And when you boarded my ship in San Fernando, you remained on the bridge. Yes? So your surprise will be the greater, Commander.

They waited; the armed guard of seamen remained behind Cameron, watching closely. Schrader said nothing further. Soon reports began to come in from the after part of the ship, were received in the wheelhouse and passed to the Captain. There was some exchange in German with the Officer of the Watch, and then Schrader passed what seemed to be the final order. The Officer of the Watch went back into the wheel-house and a moment later a syren began blaring throughout

120

the ship, an amplified sound on a rising and falling note, somewhat similar to the British air-raid warning syrens. As the syren died away, the Officer of the Watch nodded at a rating standing by a lever projecting from the after bulkhead, to port of the wheel. Cameron watched; the lever was pulled downwards and above it a red light began to glow. There was a hum of machinery from below. Schrader went to a telephone, spoke briefly into it, then came out from the wheelhouse to rejoin Cameron in the bridge wing. By now there was little stir along the upper deck. Only the routine watchkeepers were to be seen, along with a handful of seamen working under a petty officer. The electric humming stopped and there was a curious silence, a feeling as though breaths were being held all around the ship, above and below.

Schrader asked, 'Do you notice anything, Commander?'

'Yes. A slight imbalance . . . not quite that. It's as though the ship was going down a little by the stern.'

Schrader laughed. 'that is so precisely what is happening, Commander! Do you understand now?'

Cameron remembered the odd construction of the *Kaiserhof*'s stern, as seen briefly in San Fernando. Dead flat, somewhat similar to the sterns of some American warships of newer construction, yet not quite that. Stern plating that could be lifted, or perhaps lowered, or laid horizontal even, a kind of seagoing lorry's tailboard? Some sort of door, similar to the launching ramps of the big tank landing craft? Cameron said, 'I think I do, Captain. You open up the valves, flood the launch deck, trim the ship down by the stern –'

'And the little submarines . . . they emerge so easily into their natural element, like the laying of eggs by a chicken. And so fast. You will see, when the ship is low enough in the water aft.'

There was a distinct slope on the deck now. The *Kaiserhof* must be some six feet down by the stern, six feet below her marks aft. Cameron wondered about the limitations of such an exercise, how the ship would take it in anything of a sea, but no doubt that would have been covered. Not much use if

121

the midget submarines could be launched only in fair weather.

'You see now,' Schrader said. He pointed aft. A dark grey shape was appearing behind the *Kaiserhof*'s stern, a shape like a stubby cigar, a U-boat in miniature. One officer was seen standing in the small conning-tower, little more really than a guardrail round a hatch, body bent to a voice-pipe as the midget craft came round the stern and headed in a westerly direction. It was followed by another, then another, their courses set behind the flotilla leader. More and more . . . Cameron's count was forty-nine. The *Kaiserhof* had laid her eggs. There was a dull thud and a tremor as the stern doors were shut behind them. They moved away on the surface, their diesels leaving a blue haze of exhaust gases behind them as they steered into the lowering sun, moving to their stations to spread destruction among the convoys further out in the Atlantic. And among the ships of the US fleet on course for the Mediterranean.

12

As the launch deck was pumped out and the ship trimmed, Cameron was taken below again. In whispers he discussed his experience with Hanbury and Penrose. Penrose asked, 'Do they return to the ship, sir? Or make back into Cadiz?'

'Uncertain. Schrader was being circumspect. I got the impression he was leaving them to it, but I'm not sure. I believe they could enter Cadiz submerged if they had to.'

'They wouldn't get through the anti-submarine patrols in the Straits, sir.'

'Not all of them would. I think most would have a chance of getting away with it. Sheer numbers! But I don't know if that's the intention.'

Hanbury asked, 'They could be re-embarked, if that's the word?'

'Yes. Quite easily. They just move in on their motors and settle in the chocks. But one thing's for sure, and that is, Schrader won't hang about in the vicinity now he's made the launch.' It was in fact unnecessary to have made the point: the vibration throughout the ship, very noticeable in their metal prison, spoke of the ship's engines moving at full speed. Schrader certainly was not lingering. Hanbury asked if Cameron knew the course. He did not. He had been removed from the bridge before the orders had been passed, though just before leaving the upper deck he had noted a bend in the wake that indicated the ship making a turn to starboard. That didn't mean anything in particular. Schrader might simply be moving out of the area, perhaps closing the coast of Portugal, intending to return for the re-embarkation at a pre-set time. Clearly the midget submarines would have a fairly restricted range and might have to be accorded their floating harbour before their diesels stopped for want of fuel. On the other hand, there was all this new technology; they could have some fantastic range when submerged, when they would be using their batteries . . . they might in fact have little need to surface at all other than for re-charging. They might even have some sort of ability to breathe as it were, to extract the diesel fumes, thus making it possible to use the diesels submerged so they wouldn't need to re-charge batteries . . . Cameron was no submariner. Neither was Penrose, nor any of the others. Anyhow, this whole thing was a new dimension in undersea warfare and probably no one but the Germans would know the answers for certain.

'There's one thing,' Cameron said. 'Fifty subs launched . . . forty-nine, rather. One got left behind with a mechanical defect. Anyway, it means nearly two hundred less men aboard this ship. You could say the odds are narrowing!'

Hanbury gave a hard laugh. There was still a ship's company of three hundred – less an unknown but possibly high number killed by the British sub-machine-guns. It left the odds very high against them. In any case, there didn't seem to be any possibility of a break-out.

But none of them had reckoned on Leading Seaman Leroy.

It was not until a little before 2000 hours that night that the Admiralty's warning signal, in cypher, was received aboard the flagship of the Task Force. It had taken time, despite arguments from the Vice-Chief of Naval Staff, to obtain authorization to break security even to an ally. The First Sea Lord would not move without the personal authority of the Prime Minister, whose pet scheme Operation Highwayman was. Mr Churchill had been engaged all day in cabinet and was not to be disturbed; and when he emerged his temper was frayed and he subjected the First Sea Lord to close and angry questioning. The American Admiral was on his bridge when the message was reported to him. Digesting it, he took a few turns up and down. In five hours he would raise Cape St Vincent. Any time between now and then he was likely to come under attack. But he had always expected he might come under attack once he had passed to the eastward of about the fortieth meridian. Attack by both aircraft and u-boats . . . but of course this was something different. Fifty of the bastards, as he remarked to the flagship's Captain, quite a number to have in among the fleet all at the one time. And small . . . that could confuse the anti-submarine crews, they might miss the echoes, think they were from a school of porpoises or something, though it was God's truth that he wouldn't neglect any echo at all from now on out. Why, he'd attack a bunch of sardines rather than risk his ships and men. But it was still a hazard.

He said, 'It's just a warning. That's *all* it is, Captain. No change indicated in the orders.'

'That,' Captain Lomas pointed out, 'would have to come from Washington. Not London.'

'Right, it would. And maybe it will for all I know, once they get the word. Meantime I have no option. We carry on. Full alertness throughout the Task Force.' He paced again, then halted, took off his uniform cap, and wiped sweat from his forehead. It was a hot night, and airless, very thick. He sensed a coming change in the weather. It didn't feel good at all. Never mind that, though. He said, 'I tell you one thing.'

'Yes, Admiral?'

'I could detach a couple of destroyers. Go ahead at full speed and try to locate these Nazi bastards. Put 'em off their stroke a little.'

'I guess that's right, sir. And the parent ship?'

'She'll have vamoosed. Or I would, if I was her captain.' The admiral paused, looking back for a moment at his heavy ships steaming solidly along astern of his shaded blue light, and at the escorts – the cruisers forming the close escort, and the destroyers the extended defence, out on either bow, on the port and starboard quarters, and steaming abeam to each side of the advance. He said, 'Orders to the *John J. Rimmer* and the *Dennison*. They're to detach immediately on full speed, keeping their course ahead – and start goddam hunting!'

They all tried to sleep. Some slept, some didn't. Cameron was too wide awake. His watch told him that the US Task Force was coming up now into the area of most danger. A/S screens were all very well but they had never stopped *everything* getting through. There would be thousands of men in those ships and what could happen didn't bear thinking about. He knew he would be at least partly responsible in that he had failed to keep his hold of the *Kaiserhof*. He wouldn't slide out of his own failure on the grounds that the Admiralty hadn't provided him with anything like enough men to do the job. So far as it went, that was certainly true, even though the intention had been to put an adequate steaming-party aboard once the cruisers ex Gibraltar had joined him. There had been a balls-up there, all right, and that was scarcely his fault, but the fact remained that he had allowed his party to be overwhelmed and now he was faced with the result.

He looked round at the men, lying about in all sorts of attitudes beneath the glaring lights. Those lights alone had become torture. And the deck was hard. Hanbury, he saw, had drifted off into an uneasy sleep; so had Cambridge, sitting back against a bulkhead with his head at an odd angle, forward and sideways, with the neck going into it like a celluloid cylinder joining the parts of a child's doll. Chief ERA Trelawney was yarning in a quiet voice to Penrose, and there was an occasional laugh from one of them. The old-style senior chief petty officers – there was no one quite like them, ashore or afloat, they were the backbone of the Navy and always had been. Almost one hundred per cent fair men to the junior ratings, solid, dependable, good-humoured and able to see the funny side when things looked black. Currently things could hardly look blacker, yet Trelawney and Penrose could manage a laugh, probably about some past service in peacetime. There was always a laugh in the Navy. You didn't have to look very far to find it.

But Leading Seaman Leroy wasn't finding anything to

laugh at. He was sitting, like Cambridge, with his back to a bulkhead and was wide awake. His eyes were staring straight in front of him, looking at nothing, seeing nothing. There was a look of total dejection and utter hopelessness. He was like living death, Cameron thought. God alone could tell what was the matter. Once again Cameron had the notion that Leroy's state of mind went beyond their current predicament. That predicament wouldn't last forever no matter what happened. Either they would be rescued, or they would bring about their own rescue, or they would finish the war in a POW camp in Germany. That would be pretty bloody but that, too, would come to an end. However, there was something about Leroy that said he was never going to come out from under his afflictions.

He couldn't be left like that.

Cameron got up and picked his way through the massed bodies to sit alongside Leroy. He asked directly, 'What is it? What's up?'

Leroy's voice was a mutter. 'Nothing, sir.'

'Come off it. Better tell me. I may be able to help.'

'Down here, sir? All shut in?'

Cameron realized that it would be useless to quote the lines about iron bars not making a cage and so on. He said, 'I take your point, but it does depend on the trouble. At least it might help to talk, don't you think?'

Leroy's mouth trembled and went a funny shape. He looked as though he was about to burst into tears. Cameron asked, 'Is it a girl somewhere?'

Leroy's face suffused. His body jerked and he stared at Cameron. A chance shot had struck the target. 'Tell me,' Cameron said quietly. 'Just tell me about it.'

'I can't. I – I bloody *can't*, sir!'

Cameron sat there a while longer, in silence. Then he said, 'Well, if you can't, you can't. I suppose. But try to cheer up. Nothing's the end of the world, you know.'

Leroy said, 'This is, for me like. Personal, like.'

Cameron kept silent. Something might emerge if he didn't force it any further, if he just sat there as a shoulder to cry on when the moment came. Then suddenly Leroy said – he seemed to blurt it out in a hurry before he changed his mind – 'I want to see the doctor, sir. There's one aboard, you know that. I want to see him. Can you see that he's told, sir?'

'Of course I can,' Cameron answered. 'No more worries, all right?' Then it hit him, right between the eyes. Leroy's curious over-reaction to the mention of a girl, and now the request for a doctor. All the hopeless looks, all the secrecy – evidently about some medical trouble that he was suffering from. It added up. Seamen were seamen. And it was nasty. There was a threat of contagion to everyone in the compartment. Cameron got up and went over to the watertight door and banged on it until the sentry opened up. Cameron insisted on Leroy's removal to the sick bay. After a good deal of delay and summoning of petty officers, Leroy was taken away and not brought back.

Cameron managed a little sleep at last. When he woke he saw by his watch that it was morning. By this time, the US Task Force would either be through into the Mediterranean or largely if not wholly beneath the Atlantic. There was no means of knowing which. Five minutes after Cameron woke, the watertight door was unclipped. Accompanied by a strong guard of seamen, Cameron saw the *Kaiserhof*'s doctor and another officer.

The doctor said in English, 'The man who reported has a venereal disease, which is contagious.'

There was a silence. The other German officer, also speaking English, said, 'All the British are filthy pigs. My Captain has been informed and has given orders. All prisoners will be taken under guard to the sick bay. The doctor is not allowed to go amongst you here.'

The officer turned away and spoke to the petty officer in charge of the guard. The British ratings, muttering about the indignity and being uncomplimentary about Leroy, were ordered out in single file. As each man went through into the alleyway, an armed German fell in behind him, with a prodding bayonet on the end of each rifle. They climbed up a number of ladders. The sick bay was situated in the superstructure at the level of the embarkation deck. It was, they found, a sizeable affair, with a surgery, a ward with twelve beds, even an operating theatre opening off the surgery. The *Kaiserhof* retained at least some of her peacetime liner amenities. Leroy was there, looking shame-faced. He didn't utter as Cameron caught his eye. All the same, Cameron saw that he wanted to communicate. More mystery. In the meantime the medical orderlies were calling the men through one by one into the ward for examination by the doctor. An armed seaman stood guard inside the door out to the deck from the surgery, another was stationed just inside the door of the ward. The remainder of the escort party was mustered on the embarkation deck outside. Leroy seemed to be signalling with his eyes at Cameron, every time he was unobserved by the Germans.

Cameron managed to get himself up alongside the leading hand as the procession moved slowly into the ward. Leroy, from the corner of his mouth and without his lips moving, whispered, 'The case of grenades, sir.'

'Yes?'

'I brought 'em out of the lorry. Shoved 'em under the tarpaulin of a boat what was lowered to the embarkation deck. The one right outside the sick-bay door. It's bin hoisted up to the davits now. I went and forgot to report. I was that worried, sir.'

Cameron gave a brief nod. The message had been understood; but how he was to reach the lifeboat was a matter of a different sort. Nevertheless, it was worth bearing in mind. Grenades . . . so near, and yet so far. They might have been found by now in any case. The examination proceeded; the doctor said there would be further examinations later, at intervals. He became heated about the disease and the undesirability of importing such things into POW camps, which in Germany were models of cleanliness and health. He didn't appear to hear when someone muttered, 'Bollocks.' He was getting to the end of his spiel when there was a sudden din from the tannoy: the action alarm blaring throughout the ship.

Away to the south of the *Kaiserhof*, not far off the Gibraltar Strait, the destroyers detached from the Task Force had run slap into a waiting group of four of the midget submarines. In the instant that the lurking killers had been picked up by the Asdics, two of them had gone into the attack and the USS *John J. Rimmer* had taken a torpedo hit just abaft her bow on the starboard side. She was well down by the head and sinking when her sister ship *Dennison*, moving under full power, dropped a pattern of depth charges that exploded right between two of the midget submarines. Although they were attacking from some distance apart, that distance hadn't been quite enough to prevent some damage to both of them; and the next pattern, as the *Dennison*, turning under full rudder, returned to the attack, came down right on target and one of the submerged midgets ceased to exist. Pieces of wreckage and a lot of diesel oil came to the surface, plus a mangled body and some German uniform – seamen's caps, jerseys and so on. As the *Dennison* turned again to take off survivors from the *John J. Rimmer* the second of the damaged pair of submarines broke surface and lay drunkenly with her bow protruding from the water and with a heavy list to starboard. Water washed over her exposed plates and a man was seen clutching a guardrail, waving and shouting to be picked up.

'Get stuffed!' *Dennison*'s captain shouted back. Then he had second thoughts: someone, somewhere would be glad enough of any information about the parent ship that had been said to be in the vicinity – he knew the British Admiralty had come up with that information to the commander of the Task Force . . . the *Dennison* carried on picking up survivors and while this was being done the two remaining midget submarines of the group the Americans had disturbed carried out another attack. The sinking *John J. Rimmer* was hit again, this time aft, there were more casualties among those who had not yet jumped into the water, and the destroyer took a sudden lurch and was gone. Two more torpedo-trails were seen streaking towards the *Dennison*. Thanks to good handling of the destroyer, both missed. Twisting and turning, pulling up short when necessary by full astern power on her

130

engines, the *Dennison* embarked the remainder of the survivors and then raced for the midget submarine, which was still afloat. Just. The destroyer stopped briefly, with her scrambling nets still lowered over her sides, and the Captain shouted for the German to get aboard.

He did so, shaking with fear and streaming blood from a gash on the head. By order of the Captain this man was taken straight to the bridge. Also on the bridge was the *Dennison*'s Chief Bosun's Mate, a Texan from Fort Worth. He was a big man, ape-like, muscular, and he hated Germans. He was ordered to take the prisoner below and find out the whereabouts of the parent ship. The *Dennison*'s captain didn't want to know how the information was obtained, he just wanted it, period. Whilst awaiting it he authorized a coded signal to the Admiral, still some distance astern, warning him positively of submarines across his track. He made a guess as to what the Admiral would do: detach more destroyers ahead and alter his own approach a little, perhaps coming up from the south rather than due west to make his run-in to the Straits.

13

The sudden sounding of the alarm rattlers had caused confusion in the *Kaiserhof*'s sick bay. The armed party of seamen were uncertain whether or not to double away to their action stations; the petty officer in charge solved their problem. Four of them were detailed to hustle the British back below, the others were to man their action positions at once. They were hastened on their way by a distant crack and the whistle of a small-calibre shell across the decks. The prisoners were pushed towards the door from the sick bay to the embarkation deck.

Once out on deck, Cameron stopped and said, 'Just a minute.'

'Move below now.' A rifle prodded into Cameron's chest. Calmly he took hold of the barrel and shifted it aside. 'You don't shoot prisoners of war. I said, just a minute.' They were now standing immediately below the boat that contained the grenades – or might still contain them. Cameron sent up a prayer that they hadn't been found. It was fifty-fifty at best. He went on, 'If there's action, I want my chaps on deck. Not locked up below. That's a reasonable request. You'd better take it to your Captain if you can't act on your own authority.'

The immediate response was an oath. Then the petty officer said, 'Orders will be obeyed. Now! Your hands above your head.'

Cameron grinned. 'Just as you say, of course.' His hands went up; so did his eyes. From then on he moved fast. Flexing his knees, he jumped, got a firm grip on a ring-bolt set in the deckhead, and swung his feet hard towards the petty officer, who was taken completely by surprise and got the full benefit of the feet on the point of the jaw. He rose a little in the air, went flying backwards across the guardrail, and toppled over the side, his rifle falling with him. Penrose and Hanbury had moved as fast as Cameron: Penrose already had a rifle seized from one of the armed seamen and was laying about him with the butt. Hanbury had jumped across to the rail and was climbing outboard of the ship's hull to join Cameron, who had now hauled himself up to the boat deck and was urgently casting off the lashings of the canvas cover of the unofficial grenade stowage. Leading Seaman Leroy and the rest of the hands had gone in fighting and, in a local sense, it was soon all over, with the Germans facing their own rifles. It couldn't last long, though they were out of sight from the bridge and the guns' crews were busy as the firing orders came down from the gunnery transmitting station. Cameron had perhaps a matter of minutes at the most. And so far, so good: the grenades were there right enough.

Hanbury appeared over the lip of the boat deck, heaving his body up. Cameron showed him the grenades. 'They should be a help,' Hanbury said. 'We can reckon on four rifles as well – next deck down. So now what do we do, sir?'

Cameron was about to answer when the after six-inch gun of the *Kaiserhof* opened, firing on a bearing off the port quarter. The discharge was followed immediately by a monumental explosion from the *Kaiserhof*'s stern and the ship shuddered violently. A blinding flash of light came, brighter than the day, and pieces of metal and strips of flesh flew over the boat deck. There were screams of agony.

Cameron said in awe, 'Must have been a direct hit on the after six-inch.'

'Yes. And any God's amount of damage – '

'Right! So we take advantage. Get all hands on the boat deck, Hanbury, fast as they can make it. We head for the bridge.'

Hanbury yelled the order down. Led by Penrose, the seamen and stokers climbed up from the embarkation deck. Mr Cambridge was with them, as though his personal safety lay now with the British. Smoke billowed out from the stern, and there was a tongue of red flame that seemed to be spreading fast. There was confusion along the embarkation deck as the German sailors rushed aft and fire hoses were dragged out and rigged. Schrader was staring aft from the port bridge wing and shouting a stream of orders. By his side was a man in Gestapo uniform, looking grim and angry. Cameron lost no time; ahead of his seamen he ran full tilt along the deck, totally unremarked from the bridge. The smoke was thick now, overlying the whole ship as a breeze from the south billowed it forward. Cameron went through it and reached the foot of the bridge ladder on the starboard side and went up fast, gesturing to Hanbury to take some of the seamen up by the port ladder. Astern, as he reached the bridge, he got a fleeting glimpse of a destroyer with the Stars and Stripes flying out along the breeze. Her guns were still in action; the for'ard guns of the *Kaiserhof* were as yet unable to bear and as Cameron, with a German rifle in his hands and two of the grenades tucked into the waistband of his trousers, went into the wheelhouse at the rush, he heard an argument in progress between Schrader and the Gestapo man. Schrader was unwilling to bring his for'ard armament to bear, since to swing the ship nearer a broadside bearing would put his ship much more dangerously at the mercy of the destroyer's gun power and torpedo-tubes. And he knew very well that the destroyer was much more manoeuvrable than his own clumsy command – and that she had the legs of him. Surrender, in fact, was in the air.

Then he saw Cameron; and saw at the same time that another of the British had knocked out the helmsman and had taken over the wheel. His face suffused; the Gestapo man reached for the revolver in a holster at his hip.

Cameron said savagely, 'Leave it.' He aimed the rifle; the revolver remained in the holster. The Gestapo man's face was contorted. Schrader seemed at a total loss. Cameron said. 'Both of you into the wheelhouse.' He gestured with the rifle. '*Move*!' At that moment Hanbury's party came up the port ladder. Schrader gave a sound of something like despair and shifted himself into the wheelhouse. The Gestapo man went through as well. Cameron detailed an AB as sentry on the chartroom's occupants and as the rating took up his post another shell smashed into the *Kaiserhof* on the port quarter, there was a heavy explosion, the ship shuddered again throughout her length and more metal flew about the decks, slivers of it cutting men down as they ran for'ard, and embedding in boats and woodwork. Smoke began issuing from holes in the funnel.

Cameron called to Penrose. 'We don't want a wreck, Chief. Look through the flag locker – the chances are they'll have a White Ensign somewhere – '

'Aye, aye, sir.' Most German ships were equipped to adopt enemy colours when they saw a need. 'Hoist right away, sir?'

'Yes.' Already the ship was in a fair way to being a shambles along the upper deck but Cameron believed she would still be seaworthy, though that last shell seemed to have penetrated and there would be some resultant chaos below – not, he hoped, in any vital part, some part that for all he could tell might be the very thing the Admiralty wanted to pull apart so as to learn its secrets. Penrose went into action fast; he raked all the signal flags out of the locker behind the wheelhouse and wireless office, strewing them about like the week's wash, and pounced on a White Ensign. He went back with it to the wheelhouse, now fully under British control.

'Here we are, sir.'

'Right! Fly it from monkey's island, Chief. We won't risk trying to reach the mainmast.'

'Aye, aye, sir. Not that the Yanks'll believe it.'

'It's all we can do. It'll give them cause for doubt, anyway.'

Penrose went up the vertical ladder from the bridge wing to monkey's island on top of the wheelhouse. Cameron could only hope the American would see the White Ensign through the thick, black smoke. Leaving the wheelhouse to Hanbury, he went out to the port wing and operated the lever of the signalling projector. The shutters clacked out the words BRITISH NAVY ABOARD. Or tried to. Cameron knew he was a lousy signalman.

Later, the Captain of USS *Dennison* confirmed this. He brought his ship up and stood off the *Kaiserhof*'s port beam, covering her with his now silent guns. Using his loud hailer, he called across.

'What the heck. Who's the communications illiterate?'

Cameron braced his body against the guardrail of the port bridge wing. 'I am. Anyway – so long as you got the message! And thanks a lot.'

'Sorry I can't stay,' came the amplified response. 'But you'd better tell me what's been going on.'

Cameron did so, and asked about the Task Force.

'Heading into danger, that's all I know till I rejoin. I got time to take you off and then sink that bastard you're on if you want?'

'I don't want. She's needed in UK.'

There was a sound of impatient incredulity from the loud hailer. 'Orders,' Cameron called back briefly. 'From on high. You can guess who.'

'Maybe I can,' the American answered. 'We have one like him too.' There was a pause. 'Look, I've made my offer. I can't go any further than that. I'll already be in the doghouse with my Admiral. I'm needed down south of here. I just hope you can cope.'

'We'll be doing our best – '

'Sure you will, and the best of luck. One thing you may not have had time to notice.'

'What?'

'Wind's backing fast. Looks like dirty weather from the north if it goes on that way.' There was a pause. 'Look, I'll spare you some hands, all right? I can put four seamen aboard you to help out, with guns. They're good in a fight but they're what you limeys call skates. Okay?'

'Fine,' Cameron said in immense relief. 'I'll send down a jumping ladder, port side for'ard.'

'They're going to send me to the chair when I get back to Norfolk, Virginia. If I get back. But you're welcome. I'll do another thing for you. I'll stand by till you've rounded up the Nazi bastards and have full control of the ship.'

136

Cameron shouted his thanks. USS *Dennison* kept her guns trained on the *Kaiserhof*. The situation was touch and go; once the American steamed away there was going to be a need for constant vigilance. For now the Germans were muted; just waiting their chance. The four US ratings embarked under the hostile stares of the German ship's company. The Americans looked around disdainfully, jaws moving on bubble-gum. So-called skates . . . they looked the part, murderers to a man as Penrose remarked *sotto voce* as they came up the jumping ladder. Their names were Cassidy, O'Toole, Barchard and Zanerewski. All of them rated seaman first class and never mind their character references. The *Dennison*'s captain could have taken the opportunity of getting rid of trouble-makers. On embarkation there had been some anti-Nazi truculence, naturally enough. One German had been hefted out of their way by an American boot that had connected hard with his crutch. All four newcomers had laughed heartily. Brought to the bridge by Penrose, they stood in a ragged line, still chewing, watching Cameron closely. Cameron was at some disadvantage in his Spanish rig; but he made the point that he was a British naval officer and currently in command of the *Kaiserhof*.

'You could've fooled me,' Zanerewski said, then ripped off a sardonic salute, forearm held horizontal from his nose before being snatched smartly to the right. He added, 'Sir.'

'I'm glad to have you with me,' Cameron said. 'I'm going to say this, though. You'll obey orders and you'll behave properly towards the German ship's company under the rules of the Geneva Convention – '

'And what's that?' Cassidy asked, grinning and nudging the man on his left.

'Don't act green with me,' Cameron answered crisply. 'Do your job and we'll get along fine. I'll keep the bullshit to a minimum,' he added. 'I recognize the fact that you're only here on temporary loan.' He brought further discussion to a halt by gesturing to the Chief ERA and ordering the re-taking of the engine spaces. Trelawney and the stokers went below, along with the US seamen and their quick-firing automatic rifles. Within the next ten minutes Trelawney had reported by telephone that he had taken over and the engine spaces had been cleared of Germans, some of whom were dead.

Cameron said, 'It's going to be a case of watch on, stop on, Chief.'

'That's all right, sir.' Trelawney would cope somehow even if he had to remain at his post all the way through to UK – a tall order but he wouldn't moan about it. It wasn't unknown in the British Navy for a ship's company to remain closed-up at action stations for a couple of days or more – but it was going to take the *Kaiserhof* a sight longer than a couple of days to reach UK, at least if the skipper meant to take her well out into the Atlantic along the normal wartime route from the Straits to home.

This was something Cameron was considering. He conferred with Chief Petty Officer Penrose. Penrose gave the obvious answer: heading west, they would be more likely to stand clear of any attack from the air – proximity to the coast of occupied France was always to be avoided when possible. Cameron nodded, walked the guarded bridge thoughtfully. When possible was the operative phrase. This time, it might not be possible; to extend the voyage gave the Germans longer to turn the tables again. Also, his own party would feel the strain badly. Then there was the question of any support force being sent out from UK as a result of Bolus' wireless signal earlier. Someone at the Admiralty might have reacted. Might: there was no knowing. If a force was on its way, which route would it take? Cameron believed the direct route was the more likely, since there would be a clear need for speed. But, of course, that depended on how the Admiralty was visualizing the *Kaiserhof*'s own likely movements.

On both sides it was a matter of guesswork. With the w/t out of action Cameron couldn't make contact with the Admiralty, with Flag Officer Gibraltar or with anyone else for that matter. In any case it was an axiom that you didn't break wireless silence at sea. The Safe To Transmit boards were always removed from their slots at sea in wartime. By the same token Cameron couldn't ask the American to relay a call for assistance.

He made up his mind. To Penrose he said, 'We take the short route. I'll head for Plymouth Sound.'

'Aye, aye, sir,' Penrose answered, his tone non-committal. Just then the American ratings reported back to the bridge from the engine-room. Cameron ordered the rest of the German ship's company, now down to an estimated one hundred and fifty men, to be rounded up and secured below. They were to be put in the compartment recently occupied by the British; there would be just about room if they packed in tight. Very tight. The Black Hole of Calcutta wouldn't be in the same league, but it couldn't be helped. The messdecks were not secure enough – that had been proved already. Once the main body of Germans had been locked up, the ship was to be gone through with a toothcomb to ensure total clearance. The officers were to be accommodated with their men, except for the Captain. Schrader, who would know the ship better than Cameron, might be needed if the weather blew up. He would be kept under guard of an armed rating in the chartroom, right behind the wheelhouse, where there was a bunk for the use of the navigating officer. He should be secure enough: the only exit from the chartroom led into the wheelhouse.

'What about the Gestapo, sir?' Hanbury asked.

Cameron said, 'Yes. That's a point. I'd rather not have him with the ratings. He'd be better in isolation!'

Penrose said, 'How about the paint store, sir?'

'Secure?'

'Very, sir. I've been down. No way out, not once the door's clipped down. Probably puke his guts up,' he added with a grin.

Cameron nodded. 'All right, the paint store.' It would be highly uncomfortable in anything of a sea and might do the Gestapo man a power of good. Seasick people often didn't think too clearly and it could soften the fellow up. Jahn was removed from the chartroom and the armed parties started about their business, herding the Germans together under the big threat of the *Dennison*'s armament. When Leading

Seaman Leroy came to the bridge to report all Germans below and locked in, Cameron called across to the American destroyer. Her Captain waved an arm in acknowledgement and at once put his engines ahead and his helm hard over to port. The *Kaiserhof* steamed on, into the beginnings of a sea, the White Ensign now hauled down and the Nazi emblem flying out along the wind. Soon the American, heading south under full power, was fading astern.

It was a lonely feeling.

Soon the weather grew bleak and quickly worsened. Heavy seas broke over the fo'c'sle as the bows bit. As the head went down foaming water streamed back past the lips of the hawse-pipes, past the anchor cables and the slips and then dropped thunderously down from the break of the fo'c'sle to rush aft across the hatch covers and fetch up against the foot of the central island superstructure. It was cold, a damp coldness that struck through to the bone in spite of the warm German clothing that Cameron had ordered to be rifled from the cabins and messdecks – duffel coats, sweaters, oilskins, seaboots. Mr Cambridge stood huddled in a corner of the starboard wing where he could when necessary relieve his seasickness directly over the side into the uncaring Atlantic. Mr Cambridge had been allocated a cabin but as the *Kaiserhof* headed towards Finisterre and the passage of the Bay of Biscay he remained in the open – he said he found the cabin claustrophobic especially when feeling so ill. He was not a young man and he looked very strained. Cameron had a word with him after a while, asking again about the vital matter that according to Cambridge overrode the bringing home of the *Kaiserhof*.

'I can't tell you that, Cameron. It's no concern of yours in any case.'

'I think it is. Considering you nearly fouled up Highwayman on account of it.'

'I've already explained that, I believe.'

'Not very satisfactorily, Mr Cambridge.'

'You'll have to wait for an explanation . . . ' Another big

sea lifted the bows, which rose into the air in a series of agonizing jerks. Cambridge was green already; this worsened his colour alarmingly. When the lift ended in momentary stillness and then the bows went down fast in a swooping motion, and at the same time the ship rolled heavily and began to imitate a corkscrew, Cambridge put his head over the side and gushed – or tried to; lack of recent food resulted in nothing more relieving than a nasty retch. He trembled from head to foot and broke out into a cold sweat. 'For God's sake . . . I'm not well, you know.'

'All right,' Cameron said. 'It'll keep a little longer.'

He went back into the wheelhouse. Penrose was taking a break below and there was an able seaman on the wheel. For a while Cameron stood by the man's side, watching the gyro repeater card. The weather was worsening fast and the visibility was coming down. The whole sea appeared covered with a tablecloth of spume torn from the breaking wave-tops, and the cloud base was low, the horizons close all round. The day was already darkening; they were in for a filthy night.

Cameron's eyelids had been drooping for some while; it was a real effort now to keep awake. But he had to keep awake. He left the wheel and walked up and down by the fore-screen windows, listening to the restless sounds, the sounds of any ship in a seaway, a creak of woodwork, vague noises from below as things shifted about in the cabins, a clatter as something fell off the chartroom table, a suddenly increased sound of machinery as the screws raced, coming clear of the water's constriction each time the ship pitched heavily and lifted the counter.

Penrose came back to the bridge, bringing a cup of cocoa. 'Raided the galley, sir. Nothing like kye to keep you going.'

'Thanks, Chief.' Cameron drank gratefully. The galley had been investigated earlier and one of the seamen, who fancied himself as a cook, had rustled up a scratch meal consisting of corned beef, heated up. It was pretty foul, but had been more or less enjoyed by all hands except Mr Cambridge, who had been unable to face it. The temporary cook had reported to Cameron on that. He had, he said, remonstrated.

'I told 'im the best thing's to eat, sir. Then there's something for the stomach to grip on to and puke up, sir – '

'Yes, quite.'

'No good, sir. Wouldn't take 'eed, sir. They never do, sir.'

'Perhaps it's just your cooking. What about the Americans?'

'Very appreciative, sir. Very appreciative indeed.'

Remembering this conversation, Cameron was wondering what form the next meal would take when Cambridge staggered in from the open bridge.

'There's a sound,' he said. 'You may not have heard it in here, Cameron. It's very distant but I believe it's aircraft.'

14

It was aircraft right enough. Cameron pressed the action alarm and passed the information to Trelawney on the engine-room telephone. He studied the lowering sky through binoculars. He could see nothing at all, though now the sound of engines was close. There was no knowing how many, but from the engine note he believed they could be Focke-Wulfs on a recce. Or more likely, considering the foul visibility or lack of it, returning from one that had been carried out in more propitious conditions further west. Convoy spotting . . . they seemed to be coming in from the west, which fitted the theory.

Hanbury was on the bridge. Cameron asked what he thought. Hanbury said, 'We can assume the Nazis'll have picked up Bolus' PL message to Gibraltar, that the ship was back in German hands. They won't know any different from that. And they'll see the Nazi ensign, if they spot us.'

'I don't think they will, not in this overcast. Not so long as they keep high, anyway.'

'Which I don't think they are somehow,' Hanbury said after a moment. Cameron fancied he was right. The engine sounds were more distinct and did indeed seem lower. Scanning the sky, he believed he saw vague shapes, something darker than the cloud. It could be an illusion. Eyes, after looking out for some time, could play tricks. Often enough in his days as an ordinary seaman on lookout from a destroyer's bridge he had seen things, or thought he had seen things, that were not there. As his binoculars swept the overcast there was a sudden commotion behind him and he

143

swung round on his heel. He saw Schrader, making a dash from the wheelhouse door on the other side of the bridge with Penrose behind him. The German captain was running for the wing. Cameron doubled in through the starboard door and ran on for the port wing. As Schrader emerged from the wheelhouse he turned and stuck out a foot. Penrose went flat. Before Cameron could reach him, Schrader had lifted something like a Verey pistol. A coloured flare shot up, breaking through the murk overhead.

'Now they will know,' Schrader said. He held up a hand as Cameron made for him, along with Penrose who had picked himself up and was looking livid. 'Please, do not attack, gentlemen. It is done. And I have done no more than my duty as a German officer. *Heil, Hitler*!'

Cameron cursed but all they could do was to wait and see what happened. Hanbury said, 'Maybe no harm's done. That flare hasn't got to mean much. Not necessarily. To the aircraft.'

'Like hell,' Cameron said. 'Look!' He pointed over the starboard bow. One of the shapes he believed he had seen was materializing into something much more solid: a Focke-Wulf – it could be positively identified now – turning to make a run across them. It came in low and roared across the bow. By this time Schrader had been removed from the bridge by Penrose, who had then come back to report that the rating on guard duty had been knocked out with his own rifle. Penrose had now jammed up the chartroom door and posted an armed guard – on the outside this time. But Schrader had already done his worst, made his point . . .

Hanbury asked, 'Open fire, sir? Close-range weapons – '

'No. Better to act innocent. It's only a recce, and the moment we open fire he'll use his w/T and report. In the meantime he may not tick over. Don't forget the German ensign.'

'Just think we let off a flare by accident?' Hanbury asked cynically.

'He just might at that.'

'Not for much longer. The bugger's signalling. Calling us up.'

Cameron swore. 'That's torn it. Unless you happen to speak German.'

'I don't. Someone else does: Cambridge.'

'By God you're right!' Cameron shouted for Cambridge, who had gone into the wheelhouse. He came out, eyebrows raised. Cameron said, 'I want you to translate when we've read the aircraft's signal, and then stand by to translate my English in reply.' He turned to Penrose. 'Chief, get Bolus here pronto, he's the morse expert even if he isn't a bunting tosser. Now, Mr Cambridge. No tricks. If that aircraft attacks, you'll be for the high jump.'

Cambridge didn't answer but his lips had tightened. Bolus came out from the w/т office. Cameron told him what was going on. The telegraphist read off the winking light, letter by letter, and Cambridge translated.

'He's asking what ship we are and why the flare.'

'Right,' Cameron said. 'Put this into German for Bolus: *Kaiserhof* under full command. Regret accidental firing of flare.'

'Is that wise?' Hanbury asked. 'To give the real name –'

'They could have recognized us, never mind that they asked our name. It pays to be honest!'

'We hope so.' Hanbury seemed unconvinced. Once again Cambridge translated and Bolus flashed the signal back, using the signalling projector in the bridge wing. They all held their breath. The FW made one more run over the decks, and then banked and flew away, making north-easterly, and they relaxed. Glancing at the chartroom port aft of the wheelhouse, Cameron saw Schrader's face. The German looked bleak.

The damage reports from Penrose were another and continuing anxiety. The USS *Dennison* had taken out the secondary steering position and as Cameron had feared after one of the American's shells had penetrated below decks, there was some structural damage. The accommodation decks – accommodation in the ship's passenger-carrying days, the state-rooms now mostly converted to offices and stores – were in

145

places open to wind and weather, but the decks were high above the waterline and the ship wouldn't take too much water unless their luck was right out. Cameron paced the wheelhouse, almost out on his feet as full dark came down. Penrose insisted on giving him a relief. 'Get your head down, sir, even if it's only half an hour. I'll call you right away if anything happens.'

It was only sensible; there would be a rocket from the Admiralty if anything should happen while the bridge was left without an executive officer in charge, but Cameron went down one deck to the Captain's quarters and turned in all standing, ready on the instant for whatever might happen. He went off almost at once and had nightmares about missing any escorts that might have been sent south to meet them. The weather was thick, in nightmare and in fact, and the ship was lurching about all over the place . . . On the bridge Penrose kept an alert watch, scorning the comparative dryness of the wheelhouse where the atmosphere was sleepifying in spite of the gunfire-shattered windows. He remained in the bridge wings, moving from side to side through the wheelhouse, thinking about the German skipper. That Verey light . . . they'd all slipped up over that. Must have been well stowed away somewhere and of course the Jerry would have known just where.

The weather was worsening from the north. Unseasonable for the time of year – very unseasonable and bloody bad luck. Penrose thought about Cameron. You couldn't go on driving yourself indefinitely, you had to crack in the end. Cameron was going to be left to sleep for a sight more than half an hour. If he didn't get a decent sleep, his judgment would suffer and all of them with it. You were always dependent on the skipper at sea, every man aboard was.

Staring out ahead, Penrose saw just blackness, no moon now, blackness filled with flying spray and solid water coming in bloody great dollops over the bow. From below there was a drumming sound now and again . . . Penrose couldn't identify it. Not bad enough to disturb Cameron . . . he called the engine-room. Stoker PO Talland answered from the

146

starting-platform.

Penrose asked, 'Where's Chiefy, eh?'

'Got 'is head down. Tucked up all nice an' comfy down by me feet – '

'Comfy my backside. I hope he's wedged in or lashed down, that's all. Hear that drumming racket, did you?'

'Yes. I reckon it's coming from the submarine stowage – '

'Could be, yes – the launch deck. The midget sub that got left behind – '

'Did it?'

'Yes,' Penrose said. 'I'll check.'

'Rightyo. I don't reckon it's lethal anyhow. Just the same, there's something else we can do, might help the general situation, like – '

'What?'

'Pray,' Stoker PO Talland said, and cut the call. Penrose knew he wasn't being funny. Cursing the short-handedness, Penrose took over the wheel and sent Able Seaman Halligon, the helmsman, below to check the launch deck. When – if – they got into Guz, that midget submarine was going to be wanted rather badly, and as intact as possible. But all was well: Halligon came back and reported all apparently secure. Penrose's thoughts went back to Stoker PO Talland. He'd had a yarn or two with Talland back in Spain and knew that he had religion. Talland was a member of the Elim Tabernacle. He looked as though he'd always led a good life, good in the sense of decent. He had that sort of face. Cheery, confident of the future – of the life beyond the earthly future, too – and somehow content. Talland would never have been one of the lads, go ashore and get stinking drunk at the first opportunity, pick up women, all that lark. Even as a young Stoker II he would never have been apprehended by the Naval patrols that kept a strict watch over the behaviour of ratings ashore. Right now, Talland would be making contact with God, not necessarily on his knees in a wildly swinging engine-room with a greasy steel deck, God wouldn't expect obeisance to the point of lunacy, but still praying. Walking the bridge again, Penrose reflected on religion as it hit men who went down to the sea in ships. It came in all sorts of guises: there were plenty like Talland, but there were the others. The Hot Gospellers, the evangelists who wouldn't let you alone once you took a passing interest but kept on producing pamphlets and unsought advice, those who went a bit barmy with it and spent their time moaning about having to live alongside sinful people and doing their best to save the souls of their shipmates, a kind of unofficial padre's mate . . . Penrose grinned to himself, recalling a book he'd read soon after the start of the war, a volume on ranks and uniforms in the German forces. They had a person known as a Feld Bischop, in other words a Field Bishop. The mind boggled . . .

Eyes: as with Cameron they played tricks. Vague shapes in the blackness, could be anything, were probably nothing. They *were* nothing. They came and went, nothing substantial. The cold crept into Penrose's bones, the cold and the wet. The drumming from below was irregular, couldn't be anything really serious. Maybe it was succumbing to prayer, bit by bit, and Talland hadn't quite got there yet, the atmospherics were bad between him and God. Penrose went into the wheelhouse and checked the course. The gyro repeater was swinging all over the show, click-click-click as the ship's head altered. The helmsman was having a difficult night of it but was doing his best and doing it well. The mean course looked all right. It was too dark now, too thick and spray-filled to see even their wake, but Penrose knew it would be far from a straight line. Well, it all helped to throw off any lurking U-boats, perhaps. Not that such were likely. Cameron, in the interest of getting home fast with his prize, had felt safe enough in ordering no zig-zag unless the weather moderated a lot. U-boats didn't operate in this kind of weather, which was a happy thought.

Mr Cambridge had gone below. He'd seemed worn out; he was no longer young. Penrose, feeling the need to hear a human voice, had a friendly word with the helmsman. 'Not long before you see the sprog, eh, Lofty?' He happened to know that Halligon had become the father of a boy just before getting his draft chit from Devonport barracks.

148

'Hope you're right, Chief.'

'Think I'm not, do you?'

Halligon wiped the back of a hand across his nose. 'Dunno, Chief. It's still a long haul yet, isn't it? You'd have thought they'd have sent an escort, something to meet us, eh?'

'Yes. Likely they have, son. We just don't know, but I reckon they will . . . this crate's supposed to be important, remember?'

'Yes. But it's a hundred to one we'll miss them, isn't it? All that bloody sea . . .'

Penrose told him not to cross his bridges but he knew Halligon was right. No radar. There had been, of course, but the American gunfire had carried away the radar mast. However, even the radar wouldn't have picked up ships that might be a hundred miles to the west for all anyone knew, even if they were there at all.

Penrose asked, 'What you going to call the sprog, then?'

'Winston, Chief. Winston George Halligon.'

Penrose hid a grin. 'Sounds about right,' he said. Winston George . . . Prime Minister and King, a good start in life. The old warhorse, Winnie – the matloes had always had a lot of time for him, looked upon him as their own really – First Lord at the start of the 1914–18 War, First Lord again at the start of this lot, quite a record. And now Prime Minister. There was no stopping Winnie and if ever the Nazis got him, the heart would go right out of Britain. Same with the King. The Sailor King who'd never wanted the job but had put his guts into it from the start and never shirked anything. Able Seaman Halligon had the right idea. Penrose hoped the nipper would live up to it. Hoped he'd live through the bloody war and all. Devonport wasn't a good place to be, not by a long chalk. Too many targets for the *Luftwaffe*.

Down on the boat deck Leading Seaman Leroy was nursing a grievance to add to his basic problem, a grievance that was very much linked in with it: he'd been on the very brink of salvation, i.e. medical treatment, when the Yanks had appeared and opened fire, after which the ship's company, and the British, had had more important things to do than treat disease. And after that, the German doctor had been locked up below and Cameron seemed to have forgotten all about medical matters. The chances were, Cameron wouldn't have let the doctor out anyway; then again, he might.

It was worth a try.

Leroy, in general charge of the upper deck and ship security *vis-à-vis* possible German escapes, an unlikely enough contingency in his view, climbed to the bridge during the morning watch. Penrose, following out his intention to let the skipper get a proper sleep, was still on watch.

Leroy came up the port ladder. 'Chief . . . '

'Yes.' Penrose was short. 'What is it?'

'I want to see Lieutenant-Commander Cameron.'

'Stone the bloody crows,' Penrose said in exasperation. 'At *this* time o' night?' It was, by the wheelhouse clock, 0435 and ungodly. 'What about?'

'Urgent,' Leroy said briefly.

Penrose ticked over. 'Oh. I see. Your privates.'

'Yes!'

'Bloody fool to go and take the risk. Some people, I don't know!'

'It's only bloody natural,' Leroy said with a flash of anger.

'All right, lad, all right, keep your hair on and don't give me any lip. It can wait till morning.'

Leroy began to shake. Penrose saw that he was in a bad way but he wasn't going to wake the skipper just for a matter of this sort. A few hours couldn't make any difference to Leroy now. He said as much. Then he added, 'I suppose you want access to the Jerry MO?'

'That's right, I do. I'm entitled.'

'You're entitled to sod-all till the skipper says so,' Penrose said sharply. 'Specially aboard a German ship –'

'That makes no bloody difference and you know it,' Leroy threw at him. 'It's me health – me future. If you can't see that–'

'Steady, Leroy. I'm not that hard. I take your point. But it's the health of others that's more important to me, them that

150

didn't dip their wicks where commonsense told them they shouldn't, right?'

Leroy didn't answer, but breathed heavily, his mouth a thin line. Penrose said briefly, 'I'll see the skipper in the morning and then I'll let you know.'

'I want to know now.'

'Well, you can't and that's flat. There's a prize to bring home, all right? That takes priority. And in any case I can't answer for what Lieutenant-Commander Cameron will do –'

'Now look, I –'

'Shut your trap and bugger off,' Penrose said, at the end of his patience now. People with no self-respect always got his goat.

'I'm not taking that –'

'If you don't obey the order, Leading Seaman Leroy, I'll have you for leaving your place of duty on the upper deck without permission.' Penrose, too, was breathing hard now, nostrils flaring. 'Now, don't let's have any more mullarkey, all right?'

Leroy's voice was high. 'Stupid bastard!'

Penrose stood very still. 'What did you say, Leroy?'

'Stupid bastard. That's what I said or 'ave you got cloth ears? Stupid bastard! I'm bloody *sick*, and you stand there like a daft silly twat pulling rank when it's a medical matter and fuck-all to do with –'

'All right, all right.' Penrose knew when he had to soothe in the interest of not worsening the situation for all hands. If Leroy went berserk, which he was now showing every evidence of doing, it wouldn't be good for anyone. There was, Penrose thought, something as much mental as venereal. 'Just calm down, take it easy. I'll be seeing the skipper, not long now. When I wake him at seven bells to hand over for the forenoon watch. Then we'll see, eh?' His voice gave no hint of what he was thinking: that never in all his many years of service had he been spoken to by a junior rating in such a manner. It rankled; but he was capable of understanding. Even though he was dead tired himself after the events of the last few days and then nearly seven hours solid on the bridge,

151

walking up and down and straining his eyes and all his senses to avoid trouble from within the ship and without. 'I'll do my best to persuade him, Leroy.' Tired he was; too tired at his age to nip aside in time when Leroy suddenly struck him.

He slipped on the wet deck planking and went down flat. One of his teeth was out and his upper lip was badly split and bleeding. He sat up, feeling groggy. 'You bloody idiot,' he said. 'This is now a court martial offence. Striking a superior officer.'

Leroy stared down, his face working. He was scared now by what he had done. He was coming to his senses a little, Penrose thought. Penrose was getting up from the deck when Cameron appeared at the head of the port ladder.

'I heard a thump,' Cameron said. He stared as his eyes grew night-accustomed. 'What's all this? Chief, you'd better get down to the sick bay.' Penrose was looking very shaken. 'We'll send down an armed party and bring out the doctor or an SBA –'

'All right for some,' Leroy broke in bitterly. 'Send for the MO for a bloody Chief PO, oh yes!'

Cameron turned on him, eyes like ice in the dim glow from the wheelhouse. 'You'll have some explaining to do, Leroy. In the meantime I advise you to say nothing you may regret later.' He was going to add something more when the drumming sound increased, very suddenly, to be followed by a hollow booming sound that sent a shiver running up and down his spine. At the same time the ship seemed to grow sluggish and her decks began to cant towards the stern, quite noticeably. As the telephone from the engine-room whined, Cameron went into the wheelhouse to answer it. Behind him, Leroy stared at Penrose, fists clenching and unclenching and a wild look still in his eyes. Cameron said, 'Bridge here.'

'Chief ERA, sir. We're going down by the stern as I reckon you'll have –'

'Yes!'

'Could be the launch deck, sir. Something's gone.'

'Launch deck flooding . . . could be coming down from the accommodation deck. How about the engine-room, Chief?'

152

Trelawney said, 'All sound so far, sir, bulkheads holding. *And* in the boiler-room according to Talland.'

'Keep me informed,' Cameron said, and put down the handset. He went back to the bridge wing and spoke to Penrose. 'Sorry . . . I'll need you to take a look below and report. Launch deck the first check point. If it's beyond our capacity, then we'll have to let the Jerries out. Humanitarian grounds as well as work-wise.'

'Yes, sir – '

'Fast as you can, then. You stay here, Leroy.'

'I – '

'You heard the order.'

Leroy seemed to bite back further comment. He was still shaking like a leaf, having now added to his worries. He had been about to say he was sorry for what he'd done to Penrose, but did officers ever bloody listen to ratings? Like heck they did! Pigs. Bloody pigs, living in luxury, boozy parties in the wardroom when in port, Wrens being provided as officers' mattresses and no worries about what *they* might catch – they were all at it, just the same as him, only they carried gold stripes on their cuffs, a prophylactic against anything. Tears of self-pity ran down Leroy's cheeks as Cameron turned his back and went into the wheelhouse to call the engine-room again. The ship was really labouring now, and shaking her tail like a pregnant duck, and the booming sound was increasing. Looking at the wheel Cameron saw that Halligon was having difficulty with the steering.

'What's up?' he asked.

'I dunno, sir. She's heavy, like. Not answering proper, sir.'

'Trouble with the telemotor gear?'

'No, sir,' Halligon answered, 'I don't reckon it's that.' In fact Cameron could hear the telemotor's response for himself. If it was working, it could be presumed that the rudder was going over in response, but the result was practically nil. Cameron took over for a minute: heavy was hardly the word, it was like moving the wheel through molten lead. They could steer, but only just. And if the fault worsened and they found themselves unable to steer at all – if they couldn't hold the

153

ship's head to the wind and sea coming down from for'ard, there was every chance they would broach-to and swing dangerously, perhaps fatally, broadside to the storm to be lashed and battered until the ship turned over.

15

Chief PO Penrose made his way back to the bridge, wet through, lurching with difficulty along the boat deck. Clawing his way up the ladder, he reported to Cameron.

'Fair shambles, sir. There's rivets sprung along the starboard side plating, and the launch doors are letting water in too.'

'How fast is it deepening?'

Penrose shrugged. 'Not all that fast, sir. Not yet. Fast enough if we can't stop it.' His face was anxious; it said that he didn't see a lot of hope. 'The Jerries, sir – '

'Yes. They'll have to come up.'

'We won't have enough hands to watch 'em all, sir.'

'I know that. But we can't manage without them now. Use all our men to guard them, Chief. The Germans will do the work – under supervision. Get the senior German petty officer up here, soon as you can.'

'Aye, aye, sir.' Penrose turned away, went back down the ladder, taking Leroy with him this time on Cameron's permission. He began shouting for the hands to muster. Cameron heard him briefly before his voice was taken by the roaring gale and carried astern. It was going to be an uphill task, to save the ship. The options were very few: if Cameron turned away from the wind, tried to run before it, he would take more water through the launch doors aft. They might go altogether if there was enough weight of wind and sea, and he believed there was – the crests of the waves, so far as he could see them, were around twenty to thirty feet in height. But if

155

he lost all steerage, then would come the appalling danger of broaching-to. True, if he tried to turn the ship out of the wind he would at one stage come broadside on, but to do that while there was still some ability to steer would be a safer course than to be taken at the mercy of the weather to fall willy-nilly into the troughs. He had just those two alternatives. Currently he saw no point in reducing speed. The ship's stem was well capable of standing up to the pounding.

Cameron freed the door of the chartroom. 'Shift the prisoner out here, Petherick,' he said to the rating on guard.

'Aye, aye, sir.' Able Seaman Petherick called through to the German officer. 'You heard the Captain. Out!' He held his rifle steady, bracing his body against the steel bulkhead as the *Kaiserhof* lurched heavily. Schrader came out into the wheelhouse, reaching for handholds as his feet slid about the deck. So far, the helmsman was managing to keep the ship's head on course – just about, though the helm was still answering only very slowly and sluggishly.

Cameron said, 'I'm asking for your help, Commander Schrader.'

'You mean you do not know what to do.'

'I'm aware of the alternatives,' Cameron said, 'but I haven't enough hands to do the basic essential – keep the water out.' He put the position squarely to the German. 'I intend using your men, under guard. I'll need co-operation. Everyone's life is on the line now, and you know it as well as I do. Well?'

Schrader stared at him. For a while he hesitated, seeming to be listening to the whine and roar of the gale, the protesting noises from what could well be a doomed ship, making up his mind to the inevitable. He asked, 'Where are we now?'

'A little north of Finisterre.'

'Nearly into the Bay of Biscay . . . '

'Yes. And the weather's worsening. You can see that for yourself.'

Schrader nodded. He said, 'What you ask for, Commander, is my parole.'

'That's right. Will you give it?'

Schrader nodded. 'Yes, I give you my parole.'

'I can trust you?'

The German drew himself up. 'I am a German officer. You have my word. Until my ship is safe, I shall co-operate. But after that, no. My parole will be withdrawn.'

'That's fair enough,' Cameron said. 'Now I'm going to ask you to pass the word to your ship's company. You'll tell them that your parole is their parole as well – that you've spoken for them all. You agree, Commander Schrader?'

'Yes. I agree.'

'Thank you.' Cameron paused, meeting Schrader's eye. In point of fact, he wouldn't trust the man very far . . . he asked, 'And Hauptmann Jahn? Is he included?'

Schrader said, 'Hauptmann Jahn is from the Gestapo.'

'I know that. But he's under your command, presumably?'

'The Gestapo . . . the Gestapo is under the command of no one except Herr Himmler himself. I cannot speak for Hauptmann Jahn, Commander.'

'Then he can speak for himself,' Cameron said. 'Petherick?'

'Sir?'

'Leave Commander Schrader to me. Go below to the paint store and bring Hauptmann Jahn up to the bridge.'

'Take my rifle, sir?'

Cameron nodded. 'I have a revolver.' There were also the grenades, which had been stowed one deck down in the German captain's cabin, now turned over to Cameron's own use. He had almost forgotten about them; they might yet come in handy if there was trouble with the German seamen, or with Hauptmann Jahn. Soon after Petherick had gone below on his errand, Penrose came back to the bridge with Hanbury and the senior German petty officer, representative of the lower deck. Schrader began speaking to the PO but was cut short by Cameron, who preferred to wait for his interpreter. He asked, 'Where's Mr Cambridge?'

'He went to his cabin a long while ago, sir,' Penrose said. 'He felt like a lie-down –'

Cameron turned to Hanbury. 'Bring him up, please.'

157

Hanbury went down the ladder and Cameron lifted an eyebrow at Penrose. 'Well, Chief?'

Penrose said, 'I tried to tell 'em the score, sir, but I haven't the lingo and I don't know what penetrated – '

'But they guessed?'

'I reckon they did, sir, yes.'

'What's your view?'

'I think they're dead scared, sir. They won't want to be put back below, that's for sure. The bulkheads of the prison compartment were already seeping a bit, not much, but enough to give the buggers a dose of the runs. They'll do what's wanted of 'em – just so long as it suits them, that is.'

'That'll have to be good enough, then. What's it like aft now?'

'That much worse, sir, but not to the point of abandoning.'

'I haven't considered abandoning,' Cameron said. 'We're going to save her. When Mr Cambridge comes up, I'm going to get him to tell the German PO that their commander's given blanket parole on behalf of all hands. The PO's to inform the hands, and make sure it sticks. If it doesn't, then Commander Schrader's in danger. If they break parole, I shall consider his parole broken too – '

Schrader, who had been listening intently, cut in. 'This you cannot do. My parole is my own. I shall insist – '

'We'll see about that. I shall feel free to do whatever I have to do to ensure the safety of the ship. That's all about it, Commander Schrader.' Cameron turned as Hanbury came in through the starboard door accompanied by Mr Cambridge. Cameron explained the situation quickly to Cambridge. He said, 'Just in case Schrader has other ideas and expresses them in German, I want *you* to tell the PO the score. All right, Mr Cambridge?'

Cambridge said, 'So you trust me now. I'm glad of that, Cameron, very glad.'

'The proof of the pudding, Mr Cambridge. We're about to eat. And I'm sorry about the two stools.' As he finished speaking, Petherick returned with the Gestapo man ahead of his bayonet. It was coincidental, but the sudden arrival of the

158

other stool seemed to put the wind up Mr Cambridge, who was now faced with committing himself finally. However, he spoke to the German PO at some length; the man looked at Schrader, apparently for confirmation, and Schrader gave a reluctant nod.

Cambridge said, 'Well, there you are, Cameron, I've passed the message.'

'Right. Tell him to get below, muster his men, tell them they've surrendered, and they'll take their orders from Chief Petty Officer Penrose. And if there are shipwrights among the Germans, they're to report personally to Penrose.'

Cameron sent Hanbury below with Penrose. Hanbury was to take charge of the armed party on guard whilst Penrose was otherwise engaged; and as a commissioned officer of the British Navy he would represent authority to the Germans. Hauptmann Jahn was to remain on the bridge. Cameron told him that he had been released only because the ship was in danger and he might have drowned like a caged rat. There was no gratitude in Jahn's face. His eyes glittered dangerously and his mouth was a thin, hard line. He even managed to look like a rat.

Cameron asked, 'Do you give your parole, Hauptmann Jahn?'

'I do not.'

'In that case you'll be held in the chartroom. You'll come out only if necessary to save your life.'

Jahn sneered. '*Heil, Hitler.*' he said. His right arm shot into the air and his heels clicked. There was no response from Schrader. Jahn marched up to him and stood staring at him. '*Heil, Hitler!*' Jahn said again.

'*Heil, Hitler.*' Schrader gave the Nazi salute. Jahn then marched up to Cambridge and repeated the adjuration.

Cambridge was uneasy, casting glances at Cameron. '*Heil, Hitler!*' Jahn almost screamed.

Cambridge lifted his arm. '*Heil, Hitler,*' he said. He was more uneasy than ever, a tic going in his cheek. Cameron gave a slight shrug. As a double agent, Cambridge had

159

presumably to comply, to keep his cover intact. But his British cover? Surely, Jahn had now revealed him to Cameron, the two stools knocking together with a vengeance? Or was Jahn merely cocking a snook at the British, showing his contempt, getting one of them to *heil* his wretched Führer? There was something more than a little odd in the air. Once again Cameron wondered about that vital business that Cambridge had spoken of, the vital affair that made it imperative for him to maintain his standing with the Germans. There were still very many doubts about Mr Cambridge . . .

Schrader spoke again, after Jahn had been taken into the chartroom. 'What do you intend to do, Commander? For my ship?'

Cameron said, 'First, we have to make her watertight.'

'Yes, yes. How?'

'I'll have to rely on your shipwrights. I'll use them to shore up where necessary. I presume you have timber for that purpose?'

'Yes. Also the collision mat, which perhaps will help if lowered outboard over the launch doors.'

'Right. After that we'll pump out.'

'A long task.'

'But one I believe we'll manage, Commander Schrader.'

'If the ship will steer, yes, perhaps.'

Cameron agreed. He asked Schrader about the steering, what might have gone wrong. Schrader said, 'This I do not know. I had taken my ship only a little way to sea – I am not as familiar with her handling and so on as would be a captain of longer experience of her. There was no fault, however, until now. It is perhaps the Spanish dockyard workers. That is all I can say.'

'Well, my Chief PO will be sorting out your engineers. We'll see what they can do.'

Schrader didn't say anything further, but it was obvious that he, too, was worried about the steering. Soon after this conversation two Germans reported to the bridge; one was an engineer officer, the other the equivalent of a British

160

electrical artificer. They were accompanied by Cameron's EA and after a word with Cameron the EA went with them into the wheelhouse to carry out an inspection of the telemotor gear from the steering position to where it linked in with what had already been checked – and, apparently, to no avail. When the inspection of the remaining linkage had been made, the EA came back to report.

'Checked right through, sir. All correct, far as we can see. Only suggestion we've come up with is something up with the rudder itself.'

'What sort of something?'

'I dunno, sir, not to be precise. Maybe the way the rudder stock's hanging from the gudgeons.'

'Something jammed?'

'Could be that, sir.'

Cameron nodded; he had tried the wheel for himself and jamming had been the sensation he'd had. He said, 'Make another check inboard. Something may show up.' More worry: if the fault was outboard, then they hadn't a hope of righting it so long as the weather lasted, it would be impossible to put men over the stern. Except as a last resort, perhaps . . . a suicide mission to save the ship. But no, they couldn't do it, not possibly. To use heavy gear, to attempt to lift the rudder on the stern post, it simply wasn't on. He might have to abandon, but he was going to hang on as long as he could. Cambridge seemed to sense his thoughts. He said, 'If the ship should go down, that would solve your problem, Cameron. Then no one would have her.'

Cameron looked at him. He said, 'She's needed in UK, Mr Cambridge.'

'Yes, certainly, I know that, but – '

'I'm going to get her in if humanly possible,' Cameron said. He was thinking that if the ship went it would solve Cambridge's problem as well. But neither his problem nor Cambridge's was the immediate issue. If the *Kaiserhof* went down, it was highly unlikely that there would be any survivors. They couldn't even send out a distress call.

Within an hour the electrical artificer reported again: no

fault inboard, anywhere along the line that anyone could find. The Germans, he said, had done their best. In the circumstances that was hardly surprising. But it left Cameron to face the fact that the only place for the trouble was indeed the hang of the rudder-blade. The feel of the helm was worse than ever; every now and again the telemotor gear whined as though in torment – or as though it was fighting a losing battle with the rudder-blade. Penrose came to the bridge with one of the German shipwrights. The shoring-up, he said, was going well, and the collision mat had helped. There would still be water coming through but the pumps were coping. On that score, he felt he had grounds for believing they would come through. But he was as anxious as Cameron about the steering, and both he and the shipwright agreed that the rudder itself was most probably the trouble.

'Maybe something gave, like the locking pintle, or the bearing pintle, even the horizontal coupling,' Penrose said, looking baffled. 'It didn't seat back properly and now it's grinding away at the pintles and gudgeons.'

'Doesn't sound too likely.' It didn't, though Cameron was well aware that it was the locking pintle that stopped the rudder jumping from the gudgeons when a ship pitched heavily, and it was true enough they'd done plenty of pitching. 'If it *is* that, it'll get worse.'

'Yes, sir. If we're right . . . well, it could go and jam up solid.'

'If we happen to jam at a moment when there's any helm on, we'll end up going round in circles.'

'But not for long, sir.'

Cameron knew just what Penrose meant. One circle could finish them off. Just one – unless Providence was in a good mood. The situation was poor; and Providence chose that moment to indicate sour intentions. The helmsman reported in a high voice: 'She won't answer at all, sir! The wheel's moving free.'

Cameron ran for the wheel.

16

With the wheel over to starboard, there was no response at all; already the bows were paying off to port and the weight of the pounding water was coming hard on the starboard bow, forcing her round. This time it was undoubtedly the telemotor gear. Something had given way under the strain of working against a jammed rudder. The wheel was moving at a touch, no resistance at all. It was like pedalling a bicycle with the chain off.

'No good, sir?' Penrose asked.

'Bloody useless! And no secondary steering left –'

'Tiller flat, sir?'

'We'll have to try it,' Cameron said. 'It's going to need pulley-hauley right there on the rudder head – and even that probably won't work.'

Penrose started towards the door to the bridge wing. 'I'll muster a party, sir. We'll have to use the Jerries.'

Cameron nodded. 'Anyone you can find.' As Penrose slid down the ladder he went to the engine-room telephone and called the Chief ERA. 'Steering's gone altogether,' he said. 'I'm trying to steer from the tiller flat. Get the EA up here as fast as you can.'

'Aye, aye, sir.' Trelawney passed the word for the EA. Already he could feel the ship heeling over. He wondered what her safe angle of heel was, when the point of no return would be reached. All that top hamper, all that freeboard to take the full batter of the wind and sea – she wasn't going to behave like a nice slim destroyer with nice low decks. It was somewhere in these waters that HMS *Captain* had gone down,

163

a great, brand-new turreted ironclad of around 7,000 tons – she'd capsized off Finisterre, back in the 1870s. There were very old pensioners still around in Pompey and Devonport who could just about remember the mess-deck talk at the time. So far as Trelawney could recall, there had been no survivors. It would have been surprising if there had been any. You didn't last long in the drink, not in rotten lousy weather anyway, when a ship turned turtle and went down fast, carrying all her boats with her, no time to get any of them away.

Trelawney remained on the starting-platform, holding tight as the deck rose beneath him, everything sharply canted. Up above loose gear was falling about, making a devil of a racket, and the booming sound was worse than ever. He didn't dare think about the launch deck now. A moment later the telegraphs from the bridge began ringing. Full ahead port, full astern starboard. The skipper was trying to steer by engines. It might work and again it might not . . .

On the bridge, Schrader didn't interfere. He could see that Cameron was doing all that could be done in the circumstances. He felt in limbo; the first consideration had to be the ship. When she was safe, then the time would come to try to regain control before his command passed into the orbit of the British Navy. They were still a long way from the channel and anything could happen before they got there. There were strong German naval forces in Brest and in Cherbourg, and the airfields were not far behind the ports. If in the meantime he was to die in the turbulent seas, he would give his life for the Fatherland, for his Führer. That would be good; that was what he had trained for, and he had no wish to grow old and senile, to dodder round the streets of Wilhelmshaven or Kiel or sit in beer gardens boring the young with half-remembered stories of past battles and honours gained years before they had been born, an ancient relic of the naval past awaiting death.

So much better to die in full vigour, and at sea, and in combat. A dead hero was always more acceptable than one who outlived his heroism. The Reich had had one of the latter: the grand old man, Field-Marshal von Hindenburg, hero of the First World War, had lingered on to become ridiculous with his stout body, proliferant moustaches, and old-fashioned spiked helmet, someone who could have been dug up from the Franco-Prussian war . . .

Schrader looked out at the spume-covered sea: the dawn was up now, thin and watery. The *Kaiserhof* was vibrating through all her plates as one engine went ahead, the other astern. It was as though the ship was a living thing, protesting at being dragged both ways at once. The manœuvre seemed to be helping, however; the sea was still on the starboard bow but Schrader believed she was being held and might not go any further to port. If the British brought her through . . . and of course she might yet slip through the German net. It had been done before – by both sides. Schrader had been navigator of the battle-cruiser *Scharnhorst* when together with the *Gneisenau* she had steamed all the way down the channel under the very noses of the stupid, half-awake British.

Schrader began to consider more closely where his present duty lay. He glanced sideways; the British rating was very watchful, with his rifle and bayonet. The man Cambridge was supporting himself against the port bulkhead of the wheel-house, looking half dead. Schrader didn't trust Cambridge. He could jump either way and he was, of course, British. But he wouldn't want to be taken back to England under armed guard, which he would be if certain things should come out. Behind Schrader in the chartroom was Haumptman Jahn of the Gestapo. Cambridge wouldn't want Jahn to talk to Lieutenant-Commander Cameron.

Below in the tiller flat, Penrose had disconnected the steering motor and with four British seamen and a dozen Germans had got tackles secured to the two yokes of the rudder head and was taking his orders by voice-pipe from the bridge. There was tremendous strain on the starboard yoke as all hands put their weight behind the tackle, like an inter-ship tug-of-war team in peacetime, with the difference that on this occasion they were pulling literally for their lives and against the sea itself. Penrose sweated blood. There must be a God Almighty jam-up somewhere below his body. But gradually, very slowly, painfully slowly, the rudder was coming round. He believed that the ship's present heading might be held, though to continue holding it by hauling first on one yoke and then the other was going to knock the stuffing out of everyone in the tiller flat before long. A man could do so much; there always came a time when he'd had it and flaked out from sheer exhaustion. Even if he carried on, muscles didn't last forever. The engine manœuvres were helping, Penrose believed, but wouldn't be enough on their own. Such manœuvres were all very well when turning short round in a flat sea, just as an aide to the rudder, or when buggering about in port. In this sort of weather, with almost no help from the rudder, it was expecting too much.

Penrose was keeping an eye on the tiller flat's gyro repeater. The clicks came slowly – but they came.

'Backs into it, lads,' Penrose called out. 'We're winning, bit by bloody bit. One-one-two . . . *heave*!' As he heaved along with the others, thoughts of home kept intruding. Elsworth . . . the missus would never forgive him if he didn't come out of this. She depended on him; he couldn't imagine her as a widow, though he should have done by this stage of the war since death was on the cards every time he went back off leave. Funny, that. Why had the thought come now? An omen? Penrose put even more guts into it, and every heave on the rope tightened a noose around Adolf Hitler's neck.

The course had come back at last to north, and once again they were butting the stem right into the sea. The encroaching dawn – it would have been full light by this time if the weather hadn't been so overcast – showed up an empty sea, spume-covered waves in every direction. It was desolate, bleak, hostile. They were now north of Finisterre and into the Bay of Biscay. Cameron had given up all hope of encountering any British ships despatched to their assistance. Somewhere in

166

the night they must have passed, with the would-be escorting warships standing well out from the bay. He had been a fool, perhaps, to have risked the short route home. On the other hand, the time element stood – stood even more now if he'd to go on steering by tiller flat and use of the engines all the way into Plymouth Sound. Like everything else in war, it had been a matter of judgment, and judgment was usually based on chance, the weighing of one risk against another. Sometimes you were lucky, other times you weren't, and if you survived to face criticism from the Admiralty, or a court martial, then your critics or prosecutors had a wonderful time sitting on their backsides in the dry and issuing a well-considered verdict, telling you just where you had gone wrong. If they liked they could take a month mulling over what you'd had to decide in seconds. Well, that was the way of it and a lieutenant-commander RNVR couldn't alter it, he had to go with the swim.

They might yet have to swim. Or try to. What in fact would happen if he had to abandon would be one, jump, two, flounder a while in the Nazi life-jackets, and three, die.

Simple, really. Didn't take long to say to oneself . . .

Cameron took a deep breath and braced his shoulders. He'd been on the verge of defeatism. He paced the wheel-house, went out into the bridge wing. The gale buffeted, but he felt there was a little less weight behind the wind. Back in the wheelhouse, he read off the barometric pressure: the glass was rising, just a fraction.

He caught Schrader's eye. He said, 'The signs are better, Commander.'

'Yes. I think so too. If we come through, then what for my ship's company?'

'Down below again,' Cameron said. 'I'm sorry, but – '

'But it is war, and you have not a choice. Yes, I understand, of course.'

'It won't be yet. We're still in danger. I'll need every man we've got until I'm sure.'

'In war, there is no sureness until the harbour is reached.'

'You mean your ships and aircraft?'

Schrader said, 'Yes, that is what I mean. You know this as well as I do, so –'

'You're as much in the dark as I am, in regard to your naval command's intentions.'

'That is true, yes. A matter of chance for both of us.'

'If they attack, you'll be on the receiving end as well.'

'But us you will not be able to trust if that happens. The parole will be at once withdrawn. This you will have thought about. I do not underestimate you. But I think that if there is an attack, then we will win, and not you, Lieutenant-Commander. For us, the danger will be temporary only.'

Cameron turned away for a moment, thoughtfully. What Schrader had said held much truth. Any attack from the air was going to develop suddenly, swooping from the low cloud base with bombs, torpedoes, machine-guns. There would be no time to put the Nazis below decks again. On the other hand, he couldn't, as he had said to Schrader, do without their assistance yet. Cleft sticks loomed. But nothing might happen – though the chances were it would. Their movements would be known by now, and the Nazis in Occupied France were very likely just waiting their moment, which would come with lightening weather. Meanwhile there was something odd in Schrader's manner, almost as though his words and warnings, his forthcoming attitude, were all leading up to something as yet unexpressed.

Cameron stopped his pacing and faced the German squarely. He said, 'If you have anything on your mind, Commander, you'd better tell me before it's too late.'

'Yes,' Schrader said after a moment. 'You are right. I ask for a word with you, in private. And for Hauptmann Jahn to be present also.'

Cameron's eye was caught by a sudden movement on the part of Mr Cambridge, a sort of automatic response, it seemed, to Schrader's request. The man pulled himself more upright, began his tic, began blinking rapidly and seemed about to utter but in fact didn't do so. His alarm, however, was only too plain. Why? The answer to that . . . it wasn't exactly obvious but the suspicions were already in Cameron's mind. There was something he had to know.

He said, 'Very well. Outside in the starboard wing, then.'

'And Jahn?'

Cameron nodded. 'Yes, all right. Under guard, of course.'

'Yes, yes. But the sentry to remain in the wheelhouse doorway so that there is privacy.'

Cameron gave orders to the rating on guard to bring out the Gestapo man. Jahn accompanied Cameron and Schrader into the open bridge wing. It was Jahn, not Schrader, who did the talking; and what he had to say was startling, something that astounded Cameron when it emerged baldly, something that Cameron was unable to co-operate with. He said as much.

'You are being like Winston Churchill,' Jahn said angrily.

'I'm flattered!'

'I refer to the obstinacy only. It is so stupid! I have –'

'I'm not authorized to make any deals with the Gestapo. I just carry out my orders, that's all.'

'And your orders are to bring the *Kaiserhof* to a British port.'

'Yes –'

'That only. No other orders.'

'I've no intention of discussing –'

'No orders in regard to Herr Cambridge.' That was true. Cambridge wasn't Cameron's pidgin – or hadn't been up to now. Cambridge was a responsibility shared between the Foreign Office and the Director of Naval Intelligence. They were welcome to him. But the Germans didn't want him to go back to UK and the basis of Jahn's suggestion had been that Cambridge could be traded for the *Kaiserhof*'s safe delivery to Britain. Jahn had explained. The situation had altered drastically for the Nazi interest. Cambridge had never been expected to show in Spain, much less aboard the *Kaiserhof*. The midget submarines, and their parent ship, were important; there was no question about that. Important to both sides, Jahn admitted ungraciously. But Cambridge was more so. Cameron asked, why hadn't Jahn kept him in his hands while the Nazis were in control of the ship, rather than send him back to be imprisoned with the British? Jahn's answer was that a hand message had been delivered aboard in German Foreign Office cypher not long before the *Kaiserhof* had been taken over by Cameron, and in the confusion of the attack he, Jahn, had found his cyphering tables to be missing when he had gone to his cabin to safeguard them. He had suspected a Spanish thief, but ultimately, some while after the German ship's company had regained control, they had been found partially burned and thrust behind some forced-draught trunking. Because of the burning, the decyphering had not been easy but when it was accomplished they had known about Cambridge – too late. Too late until now. The matter could be rectified if Cameron was willing.

Cameron asked the question direct: whose side was Cambridge on?

Jahn said, 'With double agents, which you have guessed, of course, is what he is, one never knows. One is never quite sure, it is impossible to know which side is gaining the most. A risk is taken every time they are used.'

'But he's been useful to you in the past?'

'Yes. Very useful. You, of course, would not know how useful he has been to your British intelligence. They will not have told you anything.'

'But your people have told you?'

Jahn said, 'I am of the Gestapo. At times there are things I have to know, and I am told. I do not know the overall situation of our intelligence.'

'Then Cambridge –'

'I have said already, Cambridge is important to us. Because of recent events, more important than the *Kaiserhof*. That is to say, Germany would prefer to lose the ship than lose the man to England –'

'Why? Tell me why, Jahn.'

'I have said, because of recent events. More than that – no, I shall not say –'

'Suppose Cambridge has told us already?'

Jahn said confidently, 'This he would not do. I know by the way you react that he has not done so. It would not have been open to him to have done so. Agents do not tell others –

170

except in certain circumstances. I say it again, Lieutenant-Commander: hand Herr Cambridge over to me then if attack comes from our German forces, I will myself signal by light that·they are to desist. Then you will reach England safely.'

'So will all of you, and stay there for the duration. So will Cambridge, for God's sake!'

Jahn smiled, his face twisting, his eyes glittering blackly. 'You are so stupid. So innocent, you British! If you agree to my offer, you will send for Cambridge to come to the bridge. You will not warn him, and you will allow me to go alone with him to the chartroom. This you must do quickly. Please, your answer.'

All at once Cameron saw it: it would all be in accordance with the accepted principles, if that was the word, of espionage. Cambridge, allowed no opportunity of speaking to anyone but Jahn, would be pressured into crunching the pills in his mouth and that would be that. He felt nausea rise to the back of his throat, felt a sense of shock at Nazi cold-bloodedness, Nazi arrogance and self-assurance. Gratingly he said, 'Nothing doing, Hauptmann Jahn. And that's final.'

The Nazi's shoulders rose in a shrug. 'You have your orders. Orders for the *Kaiserhof*. You must obey them. You are being offered the chance to obey. You have no orders as to Herr Cambridge. This you have admitted yourself. I advise you most strongly to think about this.'

'You can go to hell,' Cameron said savagely. He beckoned up the armed seaman. Jahn was furious and obviously amazed at Cameron's reaction: incredulously, Cameron saw that the Gestapo man had genuinely expected co-operation in order for Cameron to save the ship – and his own skin perhaps – to be able to return to the UK with his mission successfully accomplished. Jahn had had no doubts at all that an admitted double agent, a man whose loyalty was doubted, would be jettisoned. He would never have been so forthcoming otherwise . . . and now the man's face told its own story: he had said too much, and all for nothing. White-faced, Jahn was taken back at bayonet point to the chartroom. Cameron looked at Schrader.

He asked, 'Do you go along with all that?'

Schrader said, 'Yes. I am a seaman, not Gestapo, and there are things about the Gestapo that disturb me – I confess this. Yet Jahn is right. In his suggestion there is something to satisfy both sides. You should see this, and should have accepted some disagreeableness.'

Cameron turned away, still sickened by the callous proposal. He passed the word for Hanbury: the Special Branch would be more *au fait* with intrigue of this sort. When Hanbury came to the bridge, Cameron put him fully in the picture. Hanbury said, 'It stinks, of course. But if Jahn and Schrader are willing to see themselves taken prisoner with all the ship's company . . . well, what Cambridge knows must be pretty vital to Adolf, mustn't it?'

Cameron nodded. 'Remember what Cambridge said – about there being something more important than Operation Highwayman, something that overrode even that, which was why he –'

'Why he came to Spain and so on. Yes, I remember, all right! I think we have to prise that out of him for a start.' Hanbury paused. 'Look, what if there's no attack? You said Jahn would get us out from under if an attack developed.'

'Yes –'

'But if there's *not* one, then none of this applies?'

'Correct – I suppose! We just carry on to Plymouth Sound with all hands –'

'And Cambridge – unless you agree to hand him over in the meantime. I suggest we play it down, sir. A case for a degree of masterly inactivity!'

'Not entirely,' Cameron said. 'We're far from being in the clear yet. The steering's all to hell – Penrose is coping, but all hands in the tiller flat are under physical strain. We're going to have to organize reliefs and that means keeping the Germans on deck. There's a risk in that alone, the more so now the weather's moderating.'

'How's that?'

'Well, the Germans won't be so anxious about the state of the ship once she's basically safe –'

172

'They'll get in a fighting mood – yes, I take your point. And the longer we're swanning around at sea – and if the ship can't steer in the end, God knows just how long – then that increases all the risks?'

'Yes. Reading between the lines the Nazis may attack so as to dispose of Cambridge, and never mind the rest – just in case we're apprehended by a British force. If that's the case, the German ensign won't be a protection any more –'

'So what you're saying is, we go right ahead and put Cambridge under the grill – and something else too: we have to clear our own minds, right? We have, in short, to *decide*.'

'About Cambridge. Yes. What's your view, Hanbury?'

Hanbury didn't answer right away. With the wind, still strong, tugging at his hair and the German duffel-coat, he stared out across the sea, at the breaking waves that were tending now to die down and had lost their table-cloth of spume. He could see the horizons now; the visibility was improving fast and that brought its own dangers . . .

Cameron, seeing time running out, said, 'We'll have to be quick about it, Hanbury.'

'Yes. Well, I don't trust Cambridge. We know he's a double agent and I appreciate Jahn's point that no one can be really sure . . . but I'm remembering that Cambridge never reported the facts about the time of the *Kaiserhof* leaving San Fernando.'

'He covered that. Intentional, he said. All in aid of this more pressing matter.'

'Quite! That could be a load of bull. If it is, then I'm sorry, but I reckon Cambridge has to be made to chew those pills. By us.'

17

Cambridge had gone below; Hanbury went down to bring him back. Cameron paced the bridge, desperately worried about what was to come. This was no decision for a seaman to have to make. At sea you dealt with the enemy and with the weather, which could also be an enemy. You didn't make cold-blooded decisions about suicide pills. Cameron still saw Mr Cambridge as he had seen him when they had first met in Conington church. The physical oddity, the interest in monuments. Robert Cotton by Grinling Gibbons . . . those two passwords, the cloak-and-dagger that went with the Foreign Office and Naval Intelligence – or was popularly supposed to. Cameron hadn't been able really to believe in it, not deep down. The uttering of passwords was just a joke to ordinary people. But it wasn't a joke now.

Hanbury came back with Cambridge. The neck looked thinner than ever – frail. The neck that was now at his, Cameron's, mercy. Cambridge asked, 'Can I help?'

Cameron looked quickly at Hanbury, then gave Cambridge the facts. Cambridge stood very still and said almost in a whisper, 'Oh, my God.'

'You'll have to tell me everything,' Cameron said, and waited.

'I can't. You must believe me.'

'I'm going to need some proof.'

'I can't,' Cambridge said again. He was trembling, looking sick. There was a cold sweat on his face. 'You talk about proof! How can I possibly offer that?'

'I don't bloody well know!' Cameron was sweating himself

now. 'It's up to you. According to Jahn, you're vital to Germany. Or rather, what you know is. It hasn't – from Jahn's standpoint – to get to British ears – '

'Then surely your job's to get me safely into Plymouth – isn't it?'

'Yes. But I also have my orders in regard to the *Kaiserhof*. That, I was told, was vital too. I have to know which is the more vital – the *Kaiserhof* or you, Mr Cambridge. My orders from the Admiralty were clear enough. In the absence of anything to make me disobey those orders . . . don't you *see*?'

'I see your dilemma, of course.'

'Then tell me why you're so important to the Nazis.'

Cambridge said, 'I think Jahn over-estimates that. Now I suppose you'll talk about proof again. How *can* I offer it? I'm a loyal British subject, that's all I can say in my own defence, Cameron. I swear to my loyalty, I swear it on the Bible.'

'No Bible,' Hanbury said maliciously. 'That makes it easier, doesn't it?'

'You know what I mean, Hanbury.'

'Yes, maybe. Now I think you'd better tell us what you wouldn't tell us before. What is it that's so much more important that the *Kaiserhof*? Or is it just you?'

'No, it isn't.'

'Come on, then.'

'I can't tell you,' Cambridge said desperately. 'All I can say is that I have to get into Britain. I absolutely have to. One day you may be told why. But I can't tell you now.'

Hanbury said, 'Tell us something else, then. If you have to get into Britain . . . why the hell did you ever leave in the first place? You didn't have to – except for your own purposes.'

'Yes. That's it. I told you – '

'You told us you have to square your yardarm with your bosses in Berlin, give them something to retain their trust. That was all you told us.'

'Yes,' Cambridge said again. 'That was true. But there was something else, you see. It's that that I can't tell you. It *must* be told in Whitehall. I had to go to Spain to get – that

175

information to pass on. You remember Father O'Flanagan back at that farmhouse? He – he was a link in a certain chain. I had to make personal contact. The other end of the chain was in Berlin, a source close to Hitler himself, a personal contact of mine and known for what he was only to me. *At that time*, that was. Then he became known to the Gestapo, a little late for them.' Cambridge brought out a handkerchief and wiped it across his eyes. 'It's a very involved story . . . as I say, you may be told one – '

'Not one day,' Cameron said. 'Now. This message or whatever it is, for Whitehall – why not pass it to us?'

'Why should I?' Cambridge asked. 'Just so that I become expendable, no more use – and then *you* feel the need to kill me so that I can't be made to talk by the Nazis if we should be retaken and end up in Germany – '

'You've got those capsules,' Hanbury said in a flat voice. 'You don't have to talk to the Nazis. Remember?' Then he added, 'It seems to me, from what I've heard today, that Jahn already knows what your information is, and wants to stop you taking it to the UK. I'd say we've come full circle, Mr Cambridge. If you don't tell us – '

Cambridge interrupted, his whole body shaking, his face white and drawn. 'You can't trust the Gestapo, you know! Hauptmann Jahn will simply deliver you up to the enemy when the time comes. We'll all sink together. Jahn's a fanatic, you realize that? His own death means nothing to him, so long as it's to the glory of the Führer. Well, gentlemen, I'm afraid that's all I have to say. If you'll excuse me . . . I'm really not feeling very well.'

He turned away and went for the ladder down to the boat deck. Neither Hanbury nor Cameron tried to stop him. Hanbury ran a hand through his hair, then tapped his forehead meaningly. 'Poor sod. Half-way round the bend with it all if you ask me, talking bollocks, not making sense . . . of course, it's true Jahn wouldn't have got us out from under and never mind a hand-over of Cambridge. I wonder if . . . ' Then he saw Cameron's attention had gone; he was staring up into the sky to the north-east. 'What is it?'

'Aircraft,' Cameron said. 'Don't you hear them? I think this is it.'

He ran for the wheelhouse and pressed the action alarm. Along the decks the few British seamen doubled to the guns. On the boat deck the Americans, Cassidy, O'Toole and Barchard, under the orders of Seaman First Class Zanerewski, rounded up a bunch of Nazi gunners. When the Nazis made to break away to stop the guns being manned, Zanerewski, chewing bubble-gum, reckoned that parole was being broken and he opened fire from the hip, swinging his weapon in an arc. The other did the same. The Nazis went down like ninepins. In the tiller flat Penrose carried on with the pulley-hauley, keeping the Germans at work under the British rifles. He was sweating like a pig and knew that all the effort would be puny, useless, when the bridge demanded fast alterations of course. Which now they would. Following the rattlers, word came down via the voice-pipe that the ship was about to come under attack from twin-engined JU88 bombers.

'How many, sir?'

'Upwards of a dozen, Chief. Escorted by Messerschmidts.'

'Bloody good luck to us all,' Penrose said, and carried on.

On the bridge, Hanbury said, 'Well, sir?'

'Well what?'

'Release Jahn, trust him to do his stuff?'

'And kill Cambridge? Not on your life, Hanbury.'

Hanbury shrugged. 'Somehow, I thought you'd say that. It's too late now, though.'

'Too late?'

'Cambridge is dead. He just about reached the bottom of the ladder. Took my advice. Chewed his pills.'

The attack came in, sharp and vicious. British and Americans manned the close-range weapons. A heavy curtain of fire was put up. First blood went to the ship: a Messerschmidt 109 came low, spitting tracer which arced across the bridge. The aircraft was hit amidships, and exploded in a flaming ball that fell into the sea just off the port bow. A cheer went up from the boat deck. The ship moved on, Penrose working like a demon to haul the rudder head over as Cameron did his best to dodge when the bombs started dropping. As he had thought, bloody waste of effort. Might just as well steer a straight course and do what Stoker PO Talland would be doing: pray. Talland was indeed praying while he watched his boilers and gauges and handwheels. God keep us afloat for long enough to make bloody Guz. You don't want the Nazis to win, do you? Course you don't. For Jesus Christ's sake. I've got a wife and kids – but you know that, course you do, sorry . . . Talland could hear the huge explosions, the near misses, the hits. The whole ship was ringing like a bell with the reverberations, they couldn't live through this. Please God draw the buggers off before we go up . . . go up to heaven. It's not that we don't want to in a way, but not just yet.

Helpless on the bridge, out of radio communication as he had been all along, to all intents and purposes unable to steer except dead ahead for Plymouth, a hell of a long way, Cameron watched the aircraft coming in again and again. Hanbury had gone down to the boat deck now, running to replace one of the men who had died – one of the Americans, Cassidy, his head almost disintegrated. There was blood everywhere, and the damage was mounting. The for'ard six-inch had been torn from the gun-shield which, with one of the weird quirks of explosions, itself remained intact. The barrel and the breech had exploded into a shower of metal fragments that had torn their way across the bridge, into the wheelhouse. Schrader had bought it, his throat cut from ear to ear. So far the helmsman, or the man who had been the helmsman when the wheel had had power, was all right and, leaving the useless wheel, had taken over the guard on the chartroom door. The rating charged with the duty had gone the same way as Schrader. Dead as mutton, though there was a reflex twitch in both legs. Cameron believed they had all had it now. Just one hope: the escort that might or might not have been sent out from home, might or might not have reached the area. Very forlorn: too much like luck.

There was another hit for'ard: result, a gaping hole where

the cover of Number One hatch had been. Cameron waited now for the end, but it didn't come. Just a hole – the bomb had failed to go off. An answer to prayer, or some bum work in the arms factories in Essen or wherever? The ship was taking it so far and never mind that difficulty in the launch deck earlier – she wasn't getting lower in the water, not that Cameron could notice. But it didn't help much; the Nazis wouldn't go away until they saw the *Kaiserhof* was about to sink.

Abandon?

No. They'd all just get shot up in the water. He would stay till the end came . . . and meanwhile the close-range gunners were doing well. There seemed to be a little more circumspection in the actions of the German pilots now, they were keeping their distance to some extent and it was making life harder for the bomb-aimers. And still the ship steamed on. It was not all that remarkable. Cameron remembered the Malta convoys, how the great troopships had steamed serenely on between the falling bombs, emerging through great clouds of spray from the near misses. Aircraft didn't have it all their own way by any means.

Then he saw Leading Seaman Leroy.

Leroy had been in a bad way, shaking all over. It wasn't just the terrors of the bombardment, the hopeless feeling that he was going to die. It went deeper than that. He was filled to the back teeth with hatred. Cameron, Hanbury, Penrose – all of them. They all knew he was a leper, sort of anyway, and some of them had made it very plain. By now he had persuaded himself that Cameron was behind it, was egging all hands on to keep their distance from him. It was an obsession: he'd been denied treatment until it was too late. All that Cameron's fault, not letting him see the doctor earlier. Or Penrose, who hadn't wanted to pass the message to Cameron that he wanted to see him. Just because bloody Cameron was asleep . . .   Well, he could have a bloody long sleep now.

Leroy slid himself clear of the strap of a close-range weapon on the port side of the boat deck. He was right at the for'ard end; not far to go. Fast as he could make it, he ran for the ladder leading up to the central island superstructure. Two decks up he reached the Captain's quarters, immediately below the bridge and the wheelhouse. He knew that Cameron had stowed the case of hand grenades somewhere in the Captain's accommodation. He slid the outer door aside and went in, breathing hard, the wild look back in his eye. There was, as he had known, no one there. Cameron was on the bridge and there was no steward, no such luxury on an expedition like Operation Highwayman.

He hunted around, throwing things about all over the place, no ceremony. His breathing became harder, he sweated, a curious sound came from him, half a cry, half a snarl. He was going to die himself, of course, but he would probably die anyway quite soon. No ship, he reckoned, could live through the continuing attack. But he wanted a personal hit-back before the Germans killed Cameron.

He found the grenades. They had been stowed in the wardrobe in the Captain's sleeping-cabin. Leroy dragged them out, hands shaking. He removed two of them, held the levers down and drew out the pins with his teeth. With one in each hand he left the cabin and ran for the port ladder to the bridge wing, keeping his hands concealed in the pockets of his German duffel-coat, and the levers still held down. Reaching the ladder, he climbed, lurching from side to side against the guardrails as the ship rolled. He was now a human bomb. He stepped on to the bridge.

That was when Cameron saw him. Cameron asked, 'What the bloody hell are you doing up here, Leroy?'

'Wanted a word.'

'Not in the middle of action. Get back to your place of duty at once.'

'Bollocks to that,' Leroy said, hands still in his pockets, fingers still holding down the levers of the grenades. He came closer, his breathing stertorous, mouth working oddly and a fleck of foam appearing at the corners. Cameron summed up the situation fast: Leroy was at the end of his tether. He was about to go berserk. Something had to be done quickly.

180

Cameron looked aside at the armed rating guarding the chartroom door. He jerked his head and the man came forward, rifle held loosely across his chest.

Cameron said, 'All right, Leroy. Just calm down or you might get hurt.'

'Bollocks to that, too,' Leroy said. He moved closer. Cameron stood his ground. Leroy brought his hands out from the duffel coat's pockets and held up the grenades. 'Pins are out. You know the rest.'

Cameron drew a sharp breath but kept cool. He knew all right: when Leroy let go the levers, they had seventy-nine seconds if Leroy hadn't altered the fuse setting, in which case it would be less. Cameron retreated backwards towards the bridge rail, right out into the wing where he almost overhung the sea. Leroy followed, eyes narrowed now, moving like a panther. Cameron called to the man with the rifle to stand clear. No unnecessary casualties . . . and Leroy might respond better if force was withdrawn. It could have been a miscalculation to have brought the sentry into it in the first place.

Cameron watched closely. It was touch and go. Leroy must be right round the bend, over-reacting hugely to his medical trouble. Understandable perhaps: men had killed themselves over it before now, totally unable to face wives or girl friends.

Cameron said, 'Take a grip, Leroy. It's not the end of the world.'

'So you know why I'm here.'

'I've guessed.'

'It's all your fault, you bastard, If you'd done what I wanted.'

'There's still plenty of time.'

'Not for you there's not.'

As Leroy came nearer there was a silence between them, if not elsewhere. The JUs were coming in for another bombing run and once again the close-range weapons were clattering out their chorus, pumping lead into the sky. The sentry was hovering, uncertain as to what he should do. A bullet in the back of Leroy's head might be what the skipper wanted . . .

181

but he wasn't going to shoot without orders. And Leroy was so close he might hit the skipper instead. This was an unprecedented situation, nothing laid down in King's Regulations probably. He wished desperately that the Chief PO would suddenly come up the ladder. Penrose would know at once what to do. Meanwhile, there was no order from Cameron. For his part, Cameron was unwilling to give any order at all just at the moment. The sound of his raised voice could tip Leroy right over the brink.

He said calmly, 'You'd better get on with it, Leroy. If you're going to.'

'I want you to suffer a bit,' Leroy said, 'though it still won't be as long as I've suffered.'

Cameron felt sour breath sweep his face. Leroy was very close now, fists dangling at the ends of his arms, like an ape, held slightly away from his body. Cameron took a quick look down: the levers were still held fast. Perhaps he wouldn't let them go, wouldn't do it. But Cameron believed he would. Leroy was committed now, determined to die and take Cameron with him. If he backed down, it was the end for him. Not death but worse, perhaps, in his view: that consuming disease, and a long spell in prison with hard labour. You could never, ever, get out from under a charge of threatening officers, let alone commanding officers at sea and when facing the enemy. Much more than King's Regulations and the Articles of War would be thrown at Leading Seaman Leroy. Now the sentry was approaching. Cameron mouthed at him to get back. Looking worried to death, he did so.

Cameron held Leroy's gaze. He said, 'Come on, Leroy, chuck it. You don't have to die. Throw those bloody things into the sea.'

Leroy's lips parted. There was a thin, sneering smile. He glanced momentarily up at the sky. There was some change in the overall scene, a lessening of the gunfire and aircraft sounds, but Cameron at any rate wasn't taking it in. His whole attention was on Leroy. Leroy's arms moved, the hands came up. Leroy shifted his grip and the levers sprang out from the sides of the pear-shaped killers. Cameron moved fast then,

182

diving for each wrist. He got a grip and squeezed, nails digging hard into flesh. Leroy grinned into his face and didn't let go. Sweat poured from Cameron's face. The grenades were inches away. The seconds ticked past, ticking away life, ticking towards sudden disintegration. Then Leroy made his mistake: hate seemed even at this stage to get the upper hand, hate and madness mixed. He brought up a knee and took Cameron hard in the groin, and as Cameron doubled he wrenched his arms free and stood there with the two grenades lifted. As he moved towards Cameron again, someone took his opportunity: there was a sudden stutter of fire from an automatic rifle and Leroy's taut face fell slack with a stupid look of surprise. Slowly he collapsed to the deck of the bridge wing. The grenades rolled free from his hands. Cameron dragged himself towards them, got hold of them, pulled himself to his feet and went for the side.

He threw them as hard as he could.

Just in time: they exploded in mid air and metal fragments flew. Seamen First Class Zanerewski of the US Navy came across from the head of the port ladder with his gun still smoking.

Still in pain from the knee jab Cameron said, 'Thanks.'

Zanerewski shrugged. 'Just nothing. The six-gun Navy, that's us, Captain. And you know something?'

'No . . . ' Suddenly Cameron took it in that the firing from the close-range weapons had stopped and the hands were sending up a cheer. Zanerewski said, grinning now, 'It's the Seafires, sir. Reckon your Navy Air Arm's coming in.' Within minutes the German aircraft, outnumbered and out-manœuvred, had vanished, pursued by the weaving Seafires, the Navy's equivalent of the Spitfire. Down below, Stoker PO Talland gave thanks where it was due.

Under the umbrella of the Fleet Air Arm the *Kaiserhof* steamed on towards the UK. The Seafires had come from a carrier westwards of the *Kaiserhof*'s track, detaching from a northbound convoy on orders from the Admiralty to search what had turned out to be a lucky sector. The carrier's radar had asissted, and within a matter of hours spotter aircraft had picked up the cruiser escort sent out from the Clyde and had given the German ship's position. The cruiser squadron came in at full speed from the north-west. They had not, in fact, been very far off. They made a splendid sight and a heartening one: with their destroyer escort the heavy cruisers formed up as a protective screen after putting three officers and a strong party of armed ratings aboard the *Kaiserhof*.

Thirty-six hours later, after further air attacks had been beaten off, the ship was entering Plymouth Sound. When Cameron brought her round Devil's Point and into the Hamoaze to the berth signalled by the King's Harbour Master, he found quite a reception committee waiting. No time at all was being lost; submarine experts, torpedo experts from HMS *Vernon* at Portsmouth together with the anti-submarine people, all came aboard and began ferretting about the launch deck and the disabled midget submarine that had been left behind when the flotilla had gone out on its patrol. The German prisoners were disembarked, Hauptmann Jahn being taken in a fast car under heavy escort to London along with Hanbury, who took with him Cameron's full report on events in Spain and on the voyage home. All this done, Cameron turned into his bunk, where he crashed out for the best part of twenty-four hours, after which he was woken with orders to report to the Admiralty.

'Cambridge,' a grey-haired man in plain clothes said. Cameron hadn't been told his name or function, but he was clearly from one or other of the intelligence services rather than a member of the Admiralty establishment as such. 'You'll want to know about him, of course.'

'Very much so, sir.' The interview, the debriefing, had been in progress for some while and until now there had been no specific mention of Mr Cambridge as a person, or of his death.

The grey-haired man nodded. 'Yes. Naturally, nothing that is said in regard to Mr Cambridge, or anything else you will learn, is to go any further. I quote the Official Secrets Act.

You understand fully?'

'Yes, sir.'

'In a few minutes you will go along to another room, where you will meet someone you have met before – I believe he'll be helpful to you.' The man gave a cough. 'If it hadn't been for your . . . shall I say very personal involvement with Cambridge, you would not have been told what you're going to be told. But it was thought only fair – fair to Cambridge.' There was a pause; level greenish eyes stared directly at Cameron over clasped hands. 'You believed Cambridge to have been an enemy agent.'

Cameron said, 'I knew he was a double agent.' Alarm and a sick feeling of horror had gripped him.

'But you thought more than that. However.' The man got to his feet. 'So did Hanbury. So might I had I been in your shoes. I say at once, no blame attaches to you. You did admirably. I regret that you were not more fully informed – and that's something that's down to us, not you. Now, if you'll come with me . . .'

They left the room, walked down a long, thickly-carpeted corridor, turned into another, and halted outside a heavy mahogany door. The grey-haired man pushed it open. He gestured Cameron to enter. 'I'll leave you now,' he said, and turned away.

Cameron went into the room. There was a table, two armchairs, a sideboard . . . from one of the chairs a chubby, black-clad man got to his feet, smiling, a man Cameron had never expected to see again and certainly not here. Algeciras came back, the sudden glimpse Hanbury had had of Mr Cambridge, and a priest. And then the farmhouse. . . .

'Father O'Flanagan!' Cameron said.

''Tis indeed, Commander, 'tis indeed. And glad enough to see you safe and sound.' He came forward, took Cameron's hand in both of his, then clapped him on the shoulder and went across to the sideboard. 'Whisky,' he said. 'And sit down if you please.'

Cameron dropped into the second armchair. He felt dazed; he was glad of the whisky when the priest brought the

185

glass across and said, 'It's neat. You'll not be wanting water, with a name like Cameron.' His own glass, Cameron noted, was a very full one, and also neat.

Father O'Flanagan sat down. He said, 'Cambridge was a good friend of mine, you know. A good colleague too. But you must not take this too badly, Commander. 'Tis the war's to blame and nothing else. And it ended well, as he would have wished.'

'Just tell me about it,' Cameron said. Despite the whisky, his lips felt dry.

'Right now, I will.' Father O'Flanagan sat forward, his comfortable rump on the edge of the seat. 'You see, information had come through to Mr Cambridge – you'll realize that was never his real name, of course – word passed in Spain to him that the Nazis intended to mount a cutting-out operation of their own. Naturally they had no wish for this information to be passed on, which accounts, do you see, for Hauptmann Jahn's proposal to you. I have seen your report,' he added as Cameron started to interrupt. 'I know it all, Commander. Now, I myself received word from Cadiz after your ship had left San Fernando – word that things might have gone wrong aboard. I was anxious about Mr Cambridge and his message. I too knew the content of it, you see. Because there was trouble with the communications centre at Conington Hall – the Poles, you know – I decided I had to act.'

'So you –'

'I reached London only just in time,' O'Flanagan said, smiling. 'I'll not go into how if you don't mind – routes and means that may have to be used again are best not talked about too much. Well now. Whitehall, as a result of the message, Cambridge's message, was able to reschedule things . . . to persuade the Prime Minister that it would be in the best interest of a whole lot of people if he cancelled a certain hare-brained desire to take . . . well, a certain flight in a certain aeroplane. You'll not expect me to be too precise about that, I know.'

Cameron was staring in total astonishment. 'You mean –'

'I think you've understood well enough, Commander. It

186

was Goering's own concept, all planned, all worked out to the last second and all that. I think we can both imagine what would have happened. The spirit of the country – it would have been terrible, terrible! But I think now a lesson has been learned. Tantrums will in future be firmly dealt with by the Chiefs of Staff.' Father O'Flanagan drank his whisky, leaned even farther forward, and said, 'I repeat, you must not feel badly. He knew the risks as we all did. I'll simply add that he was a good man and one who'll be sadly missed at Emmanuel.'

Cameron was left with an appalling thought: that Mr Cambridge, an old man, a double agent who had grown tired and full of strain, had ended his life on a sudden impulse because he could not live with disbelief. Father O'Flanagan seemed to sense this, and in his kindly way made the point that Mr Cambridge would have believed the *Kaiserhof* was going to be taken back into German hands and that the pills were the best way out for all concerned. It was something they would never know. A few minutes later Cameron, told to report again to the grey-haired man, was back in the debriefing room. For a while they talked about Father O'Flanagan. Cameron's mind was not on the conversation; but he concentrated when the grey-haired man said suddenly, 'You know, Cameron – you'd be a useful recruit. You've touched the fringes, and with more experience . . . I'm not without influence. You've only to say the word.'

The room seemed to lift and float, to rock around Cameron. The whole thing, in retrospect, stank to heaven. Maybe the result had been good – very good for the British people, for the whole Allied war effort, that was undeniable, but the means still stank. He said, 'I'd appreciate your influence, yes.'

'Good! Then – '

'To get back to sea,' Cameron said. He almost shouted the words. That brought the interview to a sudden close. Cameron knew his tone had been rude, truculent. He didn't give a damn. He remembered, as he left the Admiralty almost unseeingly, that meeting in Conington church. The peaceful surroundings, Cambridge and his odd appearance, his almost sinister appearance that had proved so misleading, the family monuments spanning the centuries . . . Cambridge's earnestness all the way through . . . as Father O'Flanagan had said, he was going to be a loss to Emmanuel. A good man, and quiet. Cameron walked on towards a pub off Northumberland Avenue, the Sherlock Holmes, where by prior arrangement he was to meet Chief Petty Officer Penrose. Penrose was en route for Elsworth and his interrupted leave. Hanbury had already gone off on some other job and the rest of Party Highwayman had been marched to the barracks at Devonport, together with the three surviving ratings from the USS *Dennison*. There was nothing in particular to celebrate apart from a successful end to Operation Highwayman itself. The grey-haired man, before getting on to the subject of Mr Cambridge, had parted with the information that the US Task Force had been badly mauled by the midget submarines westward of the Straits and that the operation in the Eastern Med had suffered thereby; and there had been a hint, no more, that Flag Officer Gibraltar was about to carry the can for the Admiralty's falling for a red herring that had sent the cruiser escorts from Gibraltar into the Adriatic rather than hold them in support of Cameron and his party. Nothing in particular to celebrate, but Cameron and Penrose proceeded to get blind drunk and while they were doing it the radio came up with a woman singing. *'I'm going to get so lit up when the lights go up in London, I'm going to get more lit up than I've ever been before . . . and in my gin and Angosturas I'll see little pale pink Führers. . .'*

'And balls to bloody Hitler,' Penrose said.